TOMB OF THE GOD KING

JULIA TALBOT

Julia Talbot

Tomb of the God King

Cover illustration by Catt Ford

Published with permission

First electronic edition published 2006. Second electronic edition published 2018

Third edition published 2019

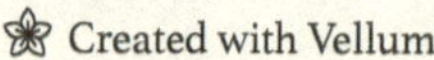 Created with Vellum

TOMB OF THE GOD KING

Englishman Christian Hewler travels to 1920s Egypt as the man Friday to an eccentric American millionaire, hoping to make history and establish his name in archaeology. What he doesn't count on is meeting brash hired gun Eric Lawless, an American cowboy working for a rival team, or the paranormal mystery that draws them in and has them facing down crazy archaeologists, dark entities, and even ancient gods.

From dark tombs to the burning-hot desert of the Egyptian landscape, Christian has to prove his mettle. During this dangerous game of cat and mouse, the reluctant partnership between Christian and Eric blossoms into more —maybe even a love that can last beyond the deception and terror hidden deep in the tombs of the Valley of the Kings.

To my wife, BA Tortuga, who encouraged me to at least put someone's eye out.

AUTHOR'S NOTE

This is a tribute to my favorite author, my favorite movie, and my love for the Cthulhu mythos. All historical liberties taken are mine and mine alone.

1

———

My only thought, as I watched two of my employer's guards become fodder for an incredibly large creature with perhaps fifty tentacles was that once I might have found such a sight odd. Now, however, the sound of men screaming and of flesh and bone rending seemed commonplace.

I should have, perhaps, begun at the beginning. The season of 1924 was unlike any I had ever attended. Thanks to the events of the previous years, the ones involving Carter and Carnarvon, Cairo proved even more difficult to navigate than usual. The Mena House seemed a veritable oasis of calm, and luckily for me, my employer had an invitation to stay there. Indeed, Mr. Alexander Royale, lately of New York, seemed to have an in to all of the correct places.

The *saffragi* lugged Mr. Royale's trunks up to his suite while I played valet. I opened one case and pulled out my employer's evening wear, for supper was to be a formal affair. Sighing at the wrinkles, I shook my head and began the arduous task of smoothing them out.

I had found, not long after joining Mr. Royale's employ,

that his idea of the duties assigned to a dig organizer and my ideas were not, in fact, the same. His ideas constituted duties as social secretary, interpreter, haggler, and indeed, dresser. Only the astonishing salary of X pounds per diem kept me from throwing the job back at Mr. Royale's protruding proboscis. That, and the opportunity to see Egypt again, which I had not done in three years.

"Be sure to shine my shoes, Christian," Royale said, appearing in the doorway. "Really, the dust here is insidious."

"Yes," I replied, unable to keep the sigh from my voice. "We're in the desert."

Mr. Royale's booming laugh rang out, and he clapped me on the back hard enough to rock me forward onto my toes. "So we are, boy. So we are."

With the sum of my experience with Americans being tied up in my employer, I could not say I found them all boorish and insensitive. Only him. One could only hope the rest were a better sort. If they were all like him, I daresay I would be forced to admit I did not like them.

I ran downstairs not long after to procure a newspaper at Mr. Royale's demand. No, the *saffragi* could not do it, he asserted. The lazy fellow would require a tip, whereas I would not.

My impression of Americans did not improve a bit on my expedition. As I entered the lounge, I endured the indignity of being knocked from my feet and onto my backside by a ruffian with no sense of decorum and an unseemly need for speed.

"Oh, beggin' your pardon, mister," the uncouth monster of a man said, his accent proclaiming his country of origin as loudly as Mr. Royale's did. "Didn't see you."

"Clearly," I returned, grunting as he hauled me up so

violently that my feet dangled for a moment before he set me down.

"Well, now, ain't you a snooty one? I apologized."

"My backside accepts," I told him. "My affronted dignity does not."

Rubbing said backside, I looked him over. The man represented the very picture of the penny-dreadful American. A long coat and a felt hat barely concealed skin as dark as an Egyptian's. His grayish eyes had fine lines cut around them, as did his mouth. They all crinkled up as the fellow smiled.

"Oh sure," he said. "You folks are all het up about your dignity, aintcha?"

"Indeed. Where yours are all about the brute force, hmm?"

Instead of taking offense as I might have hoped, the man burst out laughing, the sound booming and utterly good-natured. "You betcha. How's about we let your dignity stew on it a bit while I buy you a drink?" he asked.

In all honesty, I would have enjoyed something wet just then, so it was with true regret that I declined. "Alas, I am at work at the moment."

His eyebrows went up. "Not here, are ya? I've seen nothing but natives."

"No, I fear my American employer is staying here. And he will no doubt bellow for me any moment if I do not carry on. Good day, sir."

I made to leave him, but the fellow seized my arm in a firm grip.

"At least tell me your name so I can look you up and buy you that drink later. Make up with your dignity, so to speak."

Standing so close, I could see his eyes were not just grayish, but an unusual true gray, the ring around the iris so dark that it appeared larger than it should. His lashes, by contrast, were a dark blond. Much darker than my own silver-gilt hair that went so well with my blue eyes and the scorching Egyptian sun.

"Christian Hewler," I said. "With the Royale party."

"And I'm Eric Lawless." His hand slid down my arm to grasp and pump my own hand with a hearty shake. "I'm with Zavigny."

I had heard of Zavigny, a French excavation master known for his unconventional methods and rather crazed religious zeal. Fitting, I thought, that he should have a man named Lawless on his team.

"Pleased, I am sure." I took my hand back. "Good day, Mr. Lawless."

The man simply grinned at me, his smile wide and white against his tanned face. "See you around," he said. "Christian."

2

———

As it happened, I did not see Mr. Lawless again in the few short days we passed in Cairo. We were instead in Luxor, staying at the Winter Palace while my employer weighed the option of using his dig permit against that of renting a boat and cruising the Nile for the season instead.

I hoped rather fervently for the former, as I am not a good sailor but am an accomplished digger. It is, in fact, my passion.

Once again assisting my employer with his toilette, I listened to him ramble on, only really picking out words, when I heard him say, "Do you know, I saw that crazy Frenchman, Zavigny, today."

"Indeed?" I asked while holding up the ridiculously heavy gilded mirror Royale insisted upon traveling with.

"Yes, sir. In fact, his dig butts up on ours. Should make for a hell of a season."

Though my arms trembled with effort, I was glad he still needed the mirror to straighten his tie, for it hid my face, which no doubt showed every emotion that surged through me. Exhilaration and a savage sort of satisfaction rose chief among them. I am proud to say that my voice, when I spoke, revealed nothing.

"So we stay to dig, then?"

"We do. Zavigny thinks if we cooperate, we might find something. Hell, he's nutty as a squirrel, but he convinced me."

Then and only then did I think of the uncouth Mr. Lawless. "I hear he has American gunmen on his staff."

"Does he really? How absurd."

Royale clapped his hands, and I was able to lower the mirror, rotating my shoulders gingerly.

"Shall I hire a foreman for the dig, then?" I asked.

"Yes. See if you can get Sallah Abu Deen."

I tilted my head. "He is bound to be hired out already," I said with an impertinence that would not pass an English employer. Royale seemed to admire it. Still, it was true. Sallah Abu Deen would no doubt be out working with Carter, or perhaps Petrie. He was simply the best native foreman that money could buy.

"Then offer him more money. Are my shoes shined?"

"Yes, sir." The native boy I had hired had done a fine job at a reasonable price. If Royale's dress shoes shone that brightly, surely the slight odor of camel dung could be ignored.

"Excellent." One last yank at the tie had Royale spinning away from me, and I thought my duties might end for the night, but he turned back, his brows drawing together. "Well, get dressed, boy. I need you to attend this affair. I may need your negotiating skills."

Damnation. I could not but stare. "Surely you do not wish me to hang about lurking in your shadow?" I asked.

"Not at all. I just need you to be in the room, son. Available."

"I see. Very well. I shall meet you there anon."

"Don't dawdle, boy."

"Yes, sir."

I fear I left him feeling most affronted. I had never been accused of "dawdling" in my life. In fact, I was most accustomed to being called overly efficient. Putting my feet down hard, I made my way to the servants' wing, a holdover from the glory days of the hotel at the height of Victoria's reign.

It was there that I thought of Mr. Lawless again, or more to the point, became forcibly reminded of him as he opened the door I was reaching for and smacked me heartily in the face, as well as nearly crushing my hand.

"Lord, Mister, I sure am—oh. Well, hey there. You here to let me buy you that drink?"

Cradling my no doubt broken hand against my chest, I glared at him. "I would rather you attended to my doctor's bill. With you about, I have no doubt it will soar."

"Oh, come on now, Christian. Ain't no need to be a sorehead."

He said *head* as if it were pronounced "haid." Had I not been in pain, I might have found it charming. As it was, I chose to find it offensive.

"On the contrary, Mr. Lawless. I am sore of head, hand, and still posterior, thanks to you. I feel it is absolutely necessary."

"Suit yourself. Are you going to the ball?"

I sighed and nodded. "Sadly, yes. Royale insists."

"Well, I'll see you there, then. I was just on my way up." He tipped his hat at me and smiled, those gray eyes dancing, and I fought the urge to smack him forcibly on the nose. I imagined it would only hurt my hand.

Instead, I retaliated verbally. "Surely you are not wearing that?" I asked, wrinkling my nose to the perfect degree.

"That" consisted of a pair of wool trousers, a pair of care-worn but shined boots, a starched shirt, and a long jacket that looked more like an outdoor garment than a suit.

Lawless ran a finger around the underside of his collar, his cheeks going pink. "What's wrong with it?" he asked.

"Have you no tie?"

"Well, no."

"That will never do." Some devilish impulse had me waving him along with me. "You shall have to wear one of mine."

I felt that Eric Lawless would look as dashing and handsome in a tie as a black bear in a derby hat, and the thought pleased me endlessly. The game was on me, however, because the addition of the tie, and of pulling his hair back into a queue, made him seem utterly appealing.

Clearing my throat, I nodded. "Well, that does the trick. Off with you now, so I may dress."

"I can wait."

"No, you cannot," I said, pushing him toward the door. "I shall see you upstairs. My employer awaits."

A grimace crossed his face. "Yeah, so does mine. Now I owe you two drinks."

"I shall capitalize on that, I assure you." I would need those drinks, I was certain. "Now, go along."

Lawless finally left me to my dressing, and I swear I shook my head at myself and called myself a fool. Really, the man had nothing to recommend him. Why was I looking at him in that manner?

After dawdling as long as I could, a circumstance which had me laughing ruefully, I made my way back upstairs. The party, in full swing, caused enough noise to wake the dead, and in Egypt that possibility always seemed somehow more likely.

Mr. Royale stood among the group of sycophants surrounding Howard Carter, drink in hand, his voice rising loudly as people tried to mill away from his direction.

"Well, we all know that these rich dilettantes have the leisure to do things slowly...," Royale was saying, and I turned my back rather violently, moving toward the other side of the room.

A few old acquaintances gave me nods, one young chap who had worked with Petrie giving me a look of utter sympathy (indeed, I refused to think of it as pity). When I reached the bar, I could see why.

Several young archaeologists and assistants sat about just as I was about to, all speculating on the season to come.

"I wonder what Zavigny expects to find," one said, "out on the plot of his in the midst of nowhere."

Another shrugged. "He seems to think he has something there that predates the eighteenth dynasty by a goodly bit."

"Yes, he's crazed. The one I feel sorry for is Hewler. Working for that boorish American who waited too long to get a good permit."

That had me changing directions, and as I went along the bar, I noticed Eric Lawless sitting and staring with a morose expression into a glass of whiskey. Since I seemed as outcast as he, I took the stool next to him.

"Now would be a fine time for that drink," I said when he turned to look at me.

"Do you think my boss is insane?" Lawless asked, sounding most put-upon.

"I fear he is somewhat eccentric, but, no, I do not think he is insane. He simply has different goals than most. It could be worse. They could simply dislike him as they do my employer. Zavigny at least has the education and experience to garner pity for a fine mind gone round the bend."

"Well, we're a pair, ain't we?" Lawless waved at the barkeep, who brought another whiskey for Lawless and one for me as well.

"We are." The idea struck me as most amusing, me pairing with Lawless. He had no idea about me and would most likely beat me to a pulp had he known.

"Ah, now, old Royale I get," he said. "The Frenchie, he just has this crazy zeal."

"Perhaps we ought to switch employers," I suggested, and he burst out laughing.

"Only if you can shoot and tote heavy boxes."

"Oh, I fear I am much more useful at digging." If Royale would let me do it instead of starching his shirts.

"Old Zavigny don't let many folks do that but him," Lawless said, staring into his drink with a most thoughtful expression.

If that were the case, Zavigny's dig should progress with all the speed of a dung beetle. It amused me that Lawless pronounced Zavigny as *Zaffiggy*. Indeed, I fear it pushed me beyond my usual need for tact and diplomacy, and I had to hear it again.

"Your employer, Mr...."

"Zaffiggy," he said as I snorted into my drink. "And it's Doctor, you know. He gets real tetchy about it. What about him?"

"Has he mentioned why he is digging where he is? It seems an odd choice."

"Nope. Maybe if he had, I wouldn't think I backed a bad play." Lawless sighed, turning his glass around and around. "You want another?"

Did I? It seemed I had lost part of my good sense

already. I nodded, holding out my glass to the barkeep. I raised it and smiled. "To Dr. Zavigny!"

"Yeah, to old Zaffiggy!"

A heavy hand fell upon my shoulder just as I finished my draught, and I jumped nearly a foot as Royale's voice boomed in my ear at close range.

"I don't pay you to sit and drink with the enemy, boy," he said. "I need you to come and talk to this feller for me."

"What fellow... urk!" I vow, he grabbed me right up by the collar as if I were a naughty schoolboy and he was the headmaster. My feet hardly touched the floor when he dragged me away, and I swear I saw a flash of sympathy cross Lawless's face before Royale swung me out of sight.

"Unhand me, sir," I said. "You are embarrassing yourself."

"You mean I'm embarrassing you, you little pansy. You deserve it. What the hell are you doing? I told you I needed you close by!"

"Yes, well, clearly I was not far enough away." Suddenly face-to-face with a large party of Mr. Royale's fellow dilettantes, I staggered and righted myself when Royale let me go rather suddenly. "What was it you wished, sir?"

"Royale here tells us you dug one year with Petrie," one of the men, a blustery fellow with what I was told was a Boston accent, said.

"I did. When I was still in school." My eyes tried very hard to roll, and I stopped them by sheer force of will. It was not the first time Royale had rolled me out like a trained puppy and flashed my so-called credentials about. Amazing, how they mattered to him only when amongst his so-called peers.

"I say, does he really catalog his pottery shards as meticulously as all that?"

God save me from puerile idiots, I thought as I answered question after question. When I had taken all that I could endure, I simply folded my arms and went silent, nodding every so often while Royale held forth on how all that brushing and numbering and so on seemed pure nonsense.

He sent me away not long after like a naughty child, informing me I would not be needed again until the morrow.

Thank God.

I suppose I ought to say here that I was quite convinced of my own superiority then, especially over my poor employer, and was not so humble as I am now. I am. Truly. In fact, as I pray for my life, I find that humility comes very quickly to those who fear they are about to die.

3

I went back to the bar after I left Royale and company, ordering three whiskeys in short succession. After the third burned its way down my gullet, I felt a hand on my shoulder, this one also large and square but not demanding. When I glanced back over my shoulder, I saw Eric Lawless's tanned face and white smile.

"You look like you could use some food and some company," he said. "Wanna get out of here?"

"Yes, indeed," I returned. "Please."

"Old Royale done with you?"

"If he is not, I fear he shall have to suffer along without me." Suddenly the company of this rough American seemed far superior to that of another. At least Lawless had a winning smile and a sort of wry humor that I enjoyed. "Where shall we go to eat?"

"I say we steal a bunch of stuff from the party here and head to my room," he said, grinning so infectiously that he had me laughing with him in no time.

"Lead the way."

We stuffed our pockets, our coats, and our hands with

all manner of meats, cheeses, and desserts before I followed Lawless up a narrow back staircase to the servants' wing. His broadcloth suit coat did little to hide his broad shoulders, and I see no reason not to confess now that I admired them while I trailed behind him. They, among other things, did much to make him the attractive man he was, and I had drunk just enough that evening to be less than circumspect.

The stairs creaked under our weight, not at all like the grand staircase the guests used. Lawless's room resembled mine in every way. A small bedstead, a rickety table, and one chair populated it, and the smell of desert dust permeated every corner. Still, it was blessedly quiet, and Mr. Royale would hardly find me there.

We sat, pulling out our treats, and Lawless also pulled off his jacket, sitting in his shirtsleeves, which somehow shocked me right into silence.

"Oh," he said when all I did was to stare. "I'm sorry. Did I offend you?"

"No. No, of course not. It is your room." My cheeks heated. "Shall we try the little fish cakes?"

Ridiculous as it seemed for a man who was accustomed to seeing workers in various states of undress, the sight of Lawless in a thin linen shirt stirred me. His braces hung down behind his back, and he rolled his sleeves up before offering me a fish cake, showing the fuzz of light golden hair there. His arms flexed, hard muscle standing out, and I fairly ate my fingers instead of the fish, so intent was I upon him.

"I got something on me?" he asked, looking at his arms.

"Not at all. My, this is good bread." The flatbread was indeed tasty, with a softness I rarely encountered, as generally rations out on a dig were hardly the best. Tinned foods and hard crackers seemed the way of it for the most part.

"It's kinda flat." Appearing dubious, Lawless nevertheless laid into it, humming at the taste and giving me a pleased smile.

We ate rather companionably after that, both of us exclaiming over the pleasing little balls of meat and vegetables, both of us setting aside a particularly odd something on a skewer that tasted strongly of old boot leather. And all the while we drank from Lawless's personal store.

"Why is it you're working with Royale if you don't like him?" he finally asked after my second or third round of bemoaning my state.

"Well, you see, Mr. Lawless, I needed to come back to Egypt." I gestured with my glass, sloshing liquor about. "I *needed* to. Do you see?"

"Eric. And no, I'm afraid I don't."

"I am an excavator. I dig. Where else can I dig? And Royale was the only one who would hire me. No one in the British camps would dare after...."

I trailed of, just sentient enough of who I sat with to clamp my mouth shut.

"After what?" Those gray eyes seemed so sympathetic, though now I think there was an ulterior motive behind them. Not that I mind now, either, but then I was not looking for subterfuge.

"Well, I had something of a scandal." Whispering it conspiratorially somehow made it less humiliating.

He eyed me with obvious suspicion. "Yer pullin' my leg. You? You're awful proper for that. What'd you do, put a pot in the wrong box?"

"Hardly!" Highly affronted that he would think I could make a mistake, I carried on in high dudgeon. "My work is flawless, and I take it very seriously indeed."

"Strikes me you take everything pretty serious. So what all did you do, then?"

God help me, I had just enough spirits in me to blurt it out. "I got caught in flagrante delicto. With another man." The minute the words came out, I wished them back, but it was far too late. I sat quietly instead, waiting for him to kick me to the curb, demanding I leave his room.

"Did you now?" His expression had gone from suspicious to speculative, and his eyes twinkled at me again, as if he knew a joke and was not telling. "Well, you'd best watch yourself, then. I betcha old Royale wouldn't be too pleased to have carryings-on like that just under his nose."

"You're certainly taking this well...." Really, the last man I had accidentally confided in had socked me right in the nose.

"Well, why'n hell do you think I was smart enough to work for a Frenchie?" Lawless drawled, laughing like a loon.

I stared at him for a full minute, I swear, simply unable to believe it. "You mean, you.... I.... Well, goodness!"

My exclamation had him laughing harder, holding his stomach and just howling with it until someone nearby pounded on a wall and shouted at us in Arabic. Then he subsided for the most part, only the occasional chuckle escaping him as he wiped tears from his cheeks.

"If you could see your face," he said, still burbling. "It's the funniest damned thing."

Drawing myself up stiffly, I made to leave, weaving a bit when I stood. "I see. You were having a laugh at my expense. You are not really...." I waved my hand, unable to say the words. When I turned to go, however, he caught my arm.

Now his eyes held a completely serious, almost dangerous look. "I don't lie. I'm right fond of the less fair sex, if you get me. I figured you was too. S'why I asked you back here."

His hand felt warm, even through the layers of my coat

and shirt. Strong, with long fingers, that hand led straight to a brown wrist and hard-muscled arm that I once again could not help but notice due to the rolled-up shirtsleeve. Suddenly I wished to touch that skin, and, unwise as it seemed, I did so, reaching out with my free hand to touch the tracery of veins under the thinnest skin of his wrist.

"Is it, really?" I asked. "How extraordinary."

"Yeah? Well, maybe it is. Good thing I was right, huh?" He looked down at where I touched him, his hair falling across his forehead.

"Yes. Oh my, yes." Completely unable to resist, I moved my hand, sliding it up along his arm to feel the springy blond hairs there. "And here I thought it was because you wished to rescue me from my employer."

"Nah, that was just a good excuse." Turning, he used his hold on my arm to pull me up close, so close I could see each individual whisker on his chin, each eyelash.

Nothing short of amazing.

"Well, we should hardly waste the opportunity," I murmured, just before he bent to kiss me.

If this were one of those dreadful penny romances, I would say the birds sang and the world spun. None of that occurred. The kiss felt warm and good, Lawless's lips firm on mine, opening my mouth so his tongue could push inside. It was good, not offensive or sloppy, but it did not set the world ablaze. I fear we were both far too drunk for that.

I released Eric's arm and put both my hands on his neck, pulling him closer to taste more. The flavor of whiskey overpowered the rest, and I imagine I tasted of it as well. We kissed for long, languid moments, the heat building slowly, our bodies dulled by good food and sprits. When Lawless slid my coat off my shoulders, however, the world seemed to speed on its axis, everything moving faster, more urgently.

His sleeves slid right off over his arms, and soon enough I could stroke the muscled expanse of his chest, having disposed just as neatly of Eric's shirt. The hair there wasn't quite as light as that on Lawless's arms, leading me to believe that the man spent a great deal of time with his coat off and his sleeves rolled up. Somehow the idea of him working at some hard physical labor in the blinding sun excited me.

While I was preoccupied with his body, Eric undressed me as well, and before I could blink he pulled me to him, skin to skin. The feel of him shocked me to no end, burning off some of my inebriation. Indeed, the feel of his prick against my belly would have had me stepping back but for the arm he kept about me, holding me to him while he gave me a look that dared me to argue with him.

I did not. Especially when he kissed me again, this time tipping my head back and *taking* my mouth like a man plundering a tomb for its treasure. The languor disappeared just that quickly, and so did any lingering misgivings. I joined back in with alacrity, kissing him just as deeply as he moved back to the bed and let his weight pull us down on it.

The coverlet scratched my legs and elbows as I landed straddling his body, and I shudder to think what it must have done to his backside. He made no complaint when I pressed down against him, though, just moaned and licked at my lower lip.

He held me there, hands hard upon my skin, the palms flat as his fingers moved. It was the oddest sensation, almost ticklish, and I squirmed atop him, rubbing us together. Perhaps that was his intent, for it certainly felt marvelous.

We began to rock and I moaned, my back arching and my head pushing back. I could not even bring myself out of my own haze of pleasure enough to touch him beyond putting my hands on his chest for leverage.

I think he might have laughed at me then, a warm, throaty chuckle. "Greedy," he said.

Oh yes, I was greedy, in ways that still embarrass me to this day.

When he reached between us to touch me, I lost all control, crying out as my body bucked and jerked, my seed spending into his hand like an untrained youth.

Only then did I blink down at Lawless and realize he still moved beneath me, his skin flushed under the tan, his hips moving like mad. I slid back, sitting up on his thighs, and cupped him with both hands, listening to him moan as my fingers closed about him. Really, it was the least I could do.

The feel of his skin amazed me, so soft over such hardness. My own skin never felt so during my furtive, quick moments of pleasure. Perhaps it was simply the novelty. I had the most curious urge to bend my mouth to his skin, which I resisted, stroking him faster and faster instead, riding him as his thighs and hips bucked and shook beneath me.

When he spent himself into my hand, however, I could not stop myself from tasting his seed. I brought it to my mouth on my fingers, loving the bitterness and heat and salt.

Lawless stared up at me, eyes wide. I looked back, shocked at my forwardness and at what we had just done.

"Well," he said, his chest still heaving.

"Yes, well. I... I should get back. Royale will no doubt want a piece of my hide for leaving."

Now his eyes narrowed. "Just like that, huh? Without so

much as a thank-you or leaving two bits on the bedside table?"

My face heated almost painfully as I climbed stiffly off him. "It is not like that. I simply see no use in us pretending we were not... inebriated."

"Well, God save me from drunk Englishmen, then. Didn't think there was any harm in pretending you don't want to be well away the minute we're done."

"Please, stop." Searching, I found my clothes and dressed, feeling as awkward as a schoolboy in front of the headmaster under his look. "I'm sorry," I said. "I simply feel this was a terrible mistake."

"Then get the hell out." It came out flat and menacing, very much the voice of a cold-blooded gunman.

"Yes. Yes, of course." My last view of him was of his amazing body, sheened with sweat and seed, his face set in hard lines. I sighed. My employer was certainly right; in hindsight. Eric Lawless was the enemy now.

4

"Where in hell's name were you last night, boy?" Mr. Royale boomed at me when I attended him in his room later that morning, bringing him his newspaper and his coffee.

"I was with you at the soiree, of course." If I maintained innocence, it might fool him.

"I mean after you left. Damn it, man, I pay you to stay close."

"And I did, until it was time for me to return to my room. Even the most attentive employee must sleep." There. Let him chew on that.

"Are you being impertinent?" His bushy eyebrows lowered and his meaty hands planted on his hips.

"Why, yes, I am. I am sorry, sir, but I feel I must have some time to myself. If you cannot abide that, I can be back on a ship for England tomorrow." The threat was empty, but I imagined he did not know that, and he certainly could not get even three or four natives to do what I did for him.

He blustered a bit but finally relented. "What news on the dig? Have you gotten Sallah Abu Deen?"

"I fear not." I had not even tried, but I had managed to procure the services, just that morning, of a fine headman, one who would sit and smile as Royale shouted orders, then do what was best for the dig. "I acquired the services of Silad Mujallah. He's a fine man, and educated by your Sallah Abu Deen."

His mouth had opened, no doubt to blast me, but all he said was, "Oh."

"Yes." The mirror felt especially heavy that morning as I held it for him, possibly because he was punishing me by taking much longer than usual to get ready. "When will we set up camp?"

"Get us ready to go tomorrow. Today I am meeting with Zavigny."

My heart stuttered in my chest, but I made my voice very casual as I asked, "Oh? Why? I thought you said he was the enemy?"

"Well, we have to set boundaries, don't we, as our digs neighbor?" His cheeks went pink. "'Sides, I'm not one to turn down a free breakfast. You'll come with me, of course."

Again, my heart sank. Soon it would be in my shoes. "Of course. Just let me assume more appropriate attire." My work clothes and hat were not at all good for breakfasting at the hotel.

"Make it snappy."

Feeling long-suffering, I left him and made quick work of my ablutions and returned to him. I hoped Zavigny would not have the same policy of bringing underlings to break their fast with him.

Hope springs eternal, they say, but mine was dashed.

When we reached the breakfast room, Zavigny sat at the table, and beside him sat Lawless, looking far more presentable than I might have imagined him to be. I felt dowdy in comparison to his crisp white shirtsleeves and slicked-back hair.

"Ah, Monsieur Royale. Welcome. Please, sit. And this is your assistant, Christian, *oui*? *Bonjour*."

"*Bonjour*, Monsieur le doctor. How are you this morning?" I asked as Royale merely grunted and plopped down at the table.

Zavigny beamed at me for my manners, no doubt, and clapped his hands. "Your French accent is quite good."

"I had a fine tutor."

"I bet," Lawless said with a snort, face set and hard in the bright Egyptian morning.

"Eric! Do not be rude. You have met Monsieur Royale and Christian, no?"

"Yeah, we've had the pleasure." The sneer on the word *pleasure* made me flinch, and Zavigny's brows rose.

"I see. Well, keep a civil tongue in your head."

"Yessir."

"Now, why don't we all have some tea and order some breakfast? Monsieur, do you prefer English or continental breakfast?"

"English, please. I have to have some damned food. Buns and chocolate are for women," Royale growled.

Zavigny's cheeks went pink, but he only waved the waiter over, ordering English breakfast for three and a continental array of bread and fruit for one. Oh dear.

"Well," Royale went on, completely oblivious. "We need to set some ground rules, don't we? Since we're going to be neighbors and all."

"I would say that's a good idea. To have something to tell the workers before we even start."

That much was true. If they did not establish mutual

days of rest, the men would *fahddle* together on both camps'
rest days, losing them extra work time.

"Yes, I think that's wise," I said. "And also setting boundaries. Our camps will have to coexist, and our rock dumping
might overlap." That was always a problem in the Egyptian
desert: where to put what you dug up. Camps had gone to
war over space.

"You understand." Zavigny turned to me, smiling, while
both my employer and Eric Lawless frowned. "I have a map
here of the dispensations we both have. I think the best
place for the debris would be here."

"Oh yes," I agreed. "That would be more than fine. And
we could even have a commons area here for the men."

"I'm not paying them to loaf," Royale said, slurping his
coffee and making a face. "Damnation, get me some milk,
will you, boy?"

"You will have the men walking out if you do not give
them days of rest," Zavigny told him. "Christian has a good
plan. You ought to listen to him, *mon ami*."

"I do. But I'm the boss here, and if I say the men work
seven days a week, they work."

I shared a look with the Frenchman, his eyebrows gyrat-
ing, my eyes rolling. Royale would see how quickly work
ground to a halt when he tried to get the native workers to
work like slaves of old.

"Whatever you say, sir," I finally agreed, and that insuf-
ferable Lawless snorted.

"You sound like you actually follow orders, Limey. Too
bad we all know better."

"Eric! Am I going to have to ask you to leave?" Zavigny
truly looked scandalized, and I knew if he threw Lawless
out, I would pay for it.

I leaned forward and said in a low voice, "It is my fault,

monsieur. We had an argument yesterday, your Mr. Lawless and I, and he is still understandably sore with me."

"What could you have to argue about, boy?" Royale boomed.

"Well, sir, it was about you telling me not to fraternize with the enemy...." I simply could not resist.

"Oh."

"The enemy? La, what you must think of me."

"No, no," Royale blustered. "It was a figure of speech. I just didn't want Christian making too nice with someone not on our dig."

"Ahhh. You are jealous." One of Zavigny's eyebrows raised and lowered knowingly. "It is understandable. He is a fine specimen."

Roaring, Royale leaped to his feet, knocking his chair back. "I ain't that way. Christian, you settle everything we need with the damned Frenchman. I'll see you in an hour."

"Well, I shall have to remember that as a way to be rid of him," I said lightly, smiling at the Frenchie.

"I did not mean to offend him," Zavigny said. "I simply thought...."

"Everything offends him. More tea?"

We spent the next hour hashing out a plan that satisfied us both, giving the men two days of rest, placing the spill pile and the rest area in strategic spots. For his part, Lawless remained quite silent, his gaze as unwavering as it was unnerving.

"La," Zavigny finally said, leaning back from the table. "Eric must go and provision today. Will you accompany him?"

"I... I should check with my employer," I said at the same time that Lawless protested.

"I don't need his help."

"Eric! You are thoroughly disagreeable today. Christian, forgive him. Please, it would make me feel better if Eric had an interpreter, and I know you speak Arabic. I would happily pay you for your time."

"No, no. Royale would never stand for that. Just let me ask, and I will happily accompany Mr. Lawless."

"Happily" was stretching it, naturally, but the more I saw of the crazy Frenchman, the more I liked him, and I was willing to help.

"Well, go on, then, like a dog to his master." The look I got fair scalded me, those bright gray eyes flashing pure annoyance at me as Lawless curled his lip.

I stood, gathering my dignity about me. "I shall meet you in half an hour in the courtyard, Mr. Lawless."

Without waiting to see what else he might say, I took myself off.

He could cool his heels waiting for me. Maybe it would teach him some humility.

Though I really wasn't sure if that was possible.

5

The market was bustling, even though it was early afternoon and therefore very hot. Back in England right now, it would be damp and cold, and the question of what Eric Lawless's home might be like at this time of the year rose to my lips. Only to die when I glanced at my taciturn companion.

Clearly he was not a forgiving man.

Children ran at us from out of nowhere, ragged robes flapping and thin hands extended, cries of "Baksheesh, baksheesh!" near deafening us.

I paid the children no heed, knowing that any kind of attention might spur them on. Lawless took the mob for as long as he could before roaring and swatting at them like flies, making them giggle and run.

"You are indelicate," I said. "Some of these children might be the mayor's."

"Then he should see to it that they have something else to do." Lawless rolled his shoulders. "'Sides, I'm not the one who leaves a man right after the loving."

"Oh, for goodness' sake!" I threw my hands up, whirling

toward the stall that held pots, knowing they would need them for milk and water. "I knew it. I knew you could never be civilized about this. I cannot fathom why I even thought you could."

His hand clamped on my shoulder like a vise. "Tell me, Christian. Tell me what scared you off."

Fully intending to give him a glorious speech, I turned and opened my mouth, only to have it fall even farther open when I saw the figure behind Lawless.

Dressed in tattered beggar's robes, the thing had the gaunt, swarthy face of an Egyptian, complete with fly-ringed eyes and yellowing teeth. But the hand the man held out was not human; it was a great claw, scaly like a slithering snake, and as I backed away, it extended toward us until I thought it must surely snatch Lawless and rend him limb from limb.

It did not.

Lawless yelped as the scaly appendage touched him and was suddenly at my side, facing the beggar with his six-gun drawn.

"What the hell is that thing, Chrissy?"

"I haven't a clue." Really, I was so addled I could hardly even register the insulting nickname.

The thing shambled toward us, and I could see Lawless about to squeeze the trigger when something dropped on the ground before us and the beggar's hands turned into those of a thin man, nothing but dirty nails to fear from them at all.

My eyes felt on fire, and I blinked just enough to make sure I did not have sweat in them, distorting the image.

The beggar turned away, leaving us in a stunned tableau until finally Lawless broke the silence by clearing his throat. "Was I imagining things, buddy?"

"If you were, I had the same hallucination. How very... odd."

"Boy, you ain't just a'woofing. 'Odd' don't even begin to cover it. Should we see what he left us?"

Lawless holstered his weapon and went to squat by whatever it was the clawed man had dropped. I felt a twinge of concern for him and moved closer.

"Careful," I said. "It might be a scorpion or a snake. Some Egyptians do not care for foreigners."

"Oh, you think so?" There was no heat behind it, just a bit of breathless laughter, and Lawless poked the thing with a rock he'd picked up. "Well, it looks like some kind of canister. Maybe made of wood or bone."

"Wait! Don't touch it with your hands." If it was what I thought it to be.... Well, it might be delicate. "It looks like a scroll. Papyrus."

One light brow rose to hide under Eric's hat. "Ain't that a little rare to be tossing around at the market?"

"Indubitably. But he didn't seem your normal sort of merchant, did he?"

"Nope." I got a wide, white smile. "No dickering."

Goodness, he could be charming. That, among other things, was why I had run from him the night before. I did not wish to get to know the man and come to care about him more than I did my job. I pulled out a hankie and gingerly picked up the scroll and placed it in my pack.

"We should finish our, what did you call it? Dickering?"

"And we'll look at the scroll together after?" he asked, his gaze going from laughing to shrewd in a heartbeat.

"Yes," I agreed. "We shall."

6

———

The market seemed loud and hot, and suddenly people and flies were buzzing about where there had been strange silence. It shook me, found me looking over my shoulder while we purchased donkeys and slings, robes and tinned foods. When we finally had a store built up of what we thought Zavigny's, and my own, people would need, we hurried back to the hotel, unable to stop ourselves from striding perhaps too briskly in the heat.

I knew I must be red-faced and panting when we arrived. Lawless appeared much less affected. I had only enough time to glance his way and say, "I will meet you at your room tonight with the scroll."

"Christian! Damnation, boy! Get your ass up here and help me prepare for dinner!"

The voice was unmistakably Royale's, and I felt I needed to answer him right away, as I had been away all day and had annoyed him at breakfast to boot, but Lawless grabbed my arm.

"Promise me," he said.

"I promise. I shall not leave you waiting."

Those true gray eyes stared into mine before Lawless nodded sharply. "All right. I'll see you tonight."

I left him there, trotted up the stairs, and left my bag in the safest place I could find in Royale's room. "We are provisioned, sir."

"Wonderful. Hold my mirror."

"Yes, sir." Sighing, I hefted the heavy mirror into my hands and held it for him, feeling as though I ought to offer a bone. "About this morning, sir. I apologize heartily. Monsieur Zavigny was simply trying to be...."

"An ass. That was what he was. Hold steady, damn it."

"Yes, well. I wanted to say I was sorry if I seemed impertinent."

"Did you get all the flapdoodle ironed out? I won't talk to him about it again."

"I did. We have the site all laid out."

"Good. You can go mark it out. I'll see to setting up my tents and all." He pushed past me roughly, making the mirror shudder dangerously and making me stumble.

"I shall do that tomorrow."

"Yes. You will. And I forbid you from seeing that damnable second hand of Zavigny's again."

I stared at him as he loosened his newly tied tie. "You are not my father."

"Perhaps not, but I pay for your time. Now, go and get my hair tonic."

Feeling like a child, putting my feet down hard, I went and got his tonic and returned to help him comb it in. God, I was angry then, knowing my talents were wasted, knowing if Eric Lawless asked me to groom him so, I would, and happily, which debased me even more.

Really, I was getting to where I could hardly stand myself.

The evening dragged. Royale kept me by his side throughout, sending me running for this and that. Part of me even felt I deserved it, but I breathed a sigh of relief when he went to bed and I was able to collect my bag and the mysterious scroll and go.

A light knock on Lawless's door yielded immediate results, the portal swinging open to reveal Eric in shirt-sleeves and trousers, hair disheveled as if he had been sleeping.

"'Bout time you showed up. Get in here."

I got, stumbling into his room, which smelled of tobacco and him. Us. Musk, in other words. It had my throat going tight.

"You got it?" he asked.

"I do. Did you get what I asked for?"

"I did."

At one point during the day, I had sent Lawless a message asking him to get a piece of glass that could be cut into two, if need be. If it was a papyrus in the scroll, then the best way to preserve it once unrolled would be to press it between two panes of glass.

"Good. Shall we see what our mysterious friend gave us?"

"I been waitin' all day," Lawless snapped. "Stop teasing."

I bowed my head, feeling a strange commotion in my belly even though I knew he didn't mean it that way. My prick tried to rise in my trousers, and I sternly pushed the urge down, unwrapping the cloth I had put the scroll in.

"Well, it sure is a case. That latch thingy open it?" Lawless reached for it, and I slapped his hand away. "What? I wanna see."

"As do I, but there are sigils here that I think we ought to try to decipher first."

"You mean like a curse?" Crowding close, Lawless sneered. "You don't believe in all that, do you?"

The dampening look I gave him didn't seem to dampen him at all, for he smiled at me when I blew out a frustrated breath.

"Not really, but if it says something like, 'This scroll is infested with the venom from a thousand vipers,' we ought to think about care."

"Well then, smarty who speaks Arabic, what does it say?"

"You know that Arabic and ancient Egyptian are not one and the same, I hope." The characters were a mixture of glyphs and hieratic, as well as some sort of script I could not identify as readily.

"This says something about a pool," I said, running my finger across a line of glyphs. "As in a pool of water, deep in a tomb. And this hieratic talks about the knowledge of Those Who May See. This, though, I cannot decipher."

"Well, that don't sound all that scary."

"No, I suppose it doesn't. Here, hold this end."

While we both held gingerly to the ends of the scroll case, I undid the latch and pulled out the bottom quarter of the scroll, expecting it to crumble away to dust. That it did not surprised me, and I stared at the papyrus with a jaundiced eye.

"It must be a fake."

"Did you think the case was?"

"No, the case seems authentic enough, but this has to be new. No ancient scroll is going to look this good."

"So he wanted us to have something, then. What is it?" Lawless's breath fell upon my cheek when he leaned even closer, and I caught my own breath, trying not to let it excite me.

I looked at the scroll more carefully, unrolling the rest. "It's a map."

"X marks the spot, huh?"

"Well, not exactly. I imagine the landscape has changed a bit since this was written as well."

A sharp sigh was his answer. "Now, Chrissy, you said it was a fake."

"I think it may be a copy." Wavering, to be sure, but there was something about the map that made me think it had been real at one time.

"So where is it?"

"Somewhere in the West Valley?"

His brow furrowed even more deeply. "I thought only a few folks was buried in the West Valley."

"Well, it's true that most tombs lie in the East Valley, certainly. But this is Egypt. I never rule anything out."

"Never?"

Something in his tone alerted me, and I looked up just in time to see his face blot out the light in the room when he bent and put his lips to mine.

Startled, I jumped back, my hand going to my mouth. "What are you about?"

"I thought that was obvious," he replied, advancing.

"But this is, I mean, we have the map to decipher, and really, it's not a good idea."

"Why not? I promise, you can leave right after and pretend to be virtuous and all."

"You self-righteous bastard, I left last night because I knew it was unwise, what we did. I have never claimed false virtue." Leaving the map on the small bedside table, I stalked to him and put a hand to the middle of his chest, shoving him hard.

"No? You sure acted like you had the moral high ground

this morning with my boss." His gray eyes went dark, storms rolling in them. "He reamed me but good."

"Well, you deserved it. You were a churl this morning." I poked him in the chest again. "That was why I was so upset."

"Well then," he said, putting his hands on my arms to pull me closer. "Let me apologize."

His kiss bruised me, pressing my lips back against my teeth. The sting had me gasping, had me pressing forward to get more, my arms going up about his neck. I am not good at self-denial, no, indeed.

We kissed harder and harder, his tongue invading my mouth to taste me, rubbing against my tongue in the most suggestive manner. It had my prick hardening, my hips moving in a rhythm as old as time, already too aroused to last long.

"Oh, Chrissy, you're something else."

"Stop calling me that ridiculous name."

He grinned wildly, kissing me again, backing me toward the bedstead. The sense of unreality was huge; so was the sense of déjà vu. He had herded me about last night like a sheepdog with a lamb.

Determined to take a more active role, I pushed him about and shoved him down on the bed. The studs on his shirt gave way easily, one of them dropping to the floor and rolling off under the bed. The tiny *ping* distracted me just enough that he could grab my bottom and pull me up against him, his teeth sharp and hard at my throat.

"Stop. I want to get these off." Tugging at his shirt, I managed to get the thin linen off his shoulders, baring his not-inconsiderable charms. The planes of his chest fascinated me, and I traced them with my fingers, the difference between rough hair and soft skin utterly lovely. His nipples stood in hard little points, stiff and hot.

I touched those little bits of flesh, rubbing my thumbs over them and smiling when he gasped for me. "Yes. Oh, that's lovely."

"Decided to invest fully tonight, did you?"

"I invested full last night as long as we still... well."

"Uh-huh."

If he did not shut it quickly, he would make me angry, so I kissed him again, closing my eyes and sinking into him. The silence broke with the beating of my heart, and with his moan, shockingly deep in the sudden quiet.

I touched him wherever I could, and he struggled with my clothing. I fear I was no help, twisting and turning to taste more of him, all of him.

Finally he pinned me down with one hand, using the other to strip me nude, until I lay there exposed to him, a little shocked at the feel of it. I had not his breadth of chest or length of leg, but I represented well, with muscles built through years of digging.

"Pretty, Chrissy. Real pretty."

It seemed his turn to touch me now, which he did with a thoroughness that boded well for his digging ability. Starting at my throat, Lawless worked his way down, stroking the hollows at my collarbones, then my shoulders and down my arms. My fingers tingled when he petted my palms, clenching around his hands for a moment before he shook me off.

My chest got similar attention. Smoother than his, with less hair, but my nipples were just as sensitive, and his pinching and pulling had me squirming and groaning. The sensation shot straight to my prick, making it leap for him, and Lawless laughed.

"I'll get there soon enough, honey."

Well, I supposed *honey* was better than *Chrissy*, especially when said in that rough, needy tone of voice.

His breath tickled my neck while his hand slid down my belly, tracing the tiny trail of hairs there, his calluses catching and pulling. His mouth found the nipples his fingers had hardened for it, and he licked at them until I whimpered and begged.

I arched up, the feeling almost more than I could bear. My skin shivered and my muscles went tight, and oh, I wanted more. Now.

In the end I only got what I needed by accident. Lawless seemed intent upon teasing me, but he moved just so, and I turned at the right moment, and my prick slapped right into his palm. Oh, bliss.

Perfect bliss.

My eyes closed again, my head pushing back against the bed, and I began to ride his hand, demanding the friction I so desperately needed. Surprisingly enough, he gave it to me, pulling at my cock, his fingers closing tightly about my flesh.

My hands fisted in the sheets. As much as I longed to touch him as well, I felt selfish, greedy. Focused on my own pleasure. So I simply held on to the cotton beneath me and rode the feeling for all I was worth.

Distantly I could hear his voice, words becoming distinct one by one. "Come on, honey. Come on. Show me how much you love it."

And I did, didn't I? I spent myself into his waiting hand, my seed shooting out of me onto his skin. The top of my head felt like a volcano, and my balls emptied so I feared they would never be of any use again.

While I lay there panting, he licked his hand clean and

smiled at me, looking as triumphant as any man can. "Guess that do beat all you done to me, huh?"

Oh. Oh no. He would *not* get away with that. I heard a low sound come from my own throat, much like a growl. Then I was up and on him, slamming him back on the bed to undo his trousers.

"We'll see about that," I said, even while I bent to put my mouth on his straining flesh.

He shouted, the sound gratifying in the extreme. So was the way he squirmed, his prick leaping for me, his pulse pounding in his veins. The taste of him excited me, for all that I had just spent, making me breathe harder. Salty and deep, very much like the earth, he made it easy to warm to my task, sending me to licking and sucking him with a fervor.

The underside of his prick I gave particular attention, my tongue rubbing up and down until he began babbling, begging me for more. I gave it, licking my way down to his sacs so I could push them this way and that with my tongue.

The most extraordinary thing happened then. He grabbed my shoulders and flipped me on my back, coming to kneel astride my chest, his prick nudging my chin before he grabbed it and guided it to my lips. I opened my mouth, quite instinctively, and he took it, pressing his cock inside and starting to move, in and out, taking me as effectively as if he were inside my arse.

I grabbed his hips in my hands in a feeble attempt to control him, but I confess, deep down I loved it that he was so desperate for me that he would act so depraved. The furor of his motions raised me to heights I could only have imagined before, my prick rising again so fast that it left an ache in my belly.

Reaching down, I grabbed my swinging prick and pulled

at it even as I sucked harder, trying to open to him. My throat burned, and I had to breathe through my nose, but I took him, and when he finally shot into my mouth, it was cataclysmic. He sounded as though he were going to die.

My own prick jerked madly in my hand, and while I hardly reached the heights I believed Lawless had, I was left sated and bruised, panting through swollen lips, my hand coated with seed.

"Jesus Christ on a crutch, Christian," he said, pulling back to collapse beside me. "Where'n hell did you learn to do that?"

"In school, naturally."

"In... well, hell. They never taught us nothing like that. Course, I only went to sixth grade."

I laughed. "Yes, a bit young for those kinds of lessons...."

Sobering, he rolled up to one elbow and stroked my shoulder with his free hand. "You gonna run?"

"Right now, I am incapable. If you ask will I leave before dawn, most likely, yes. Royale has already expressed his opinion of my kind."

"Mine too. What about the map?"

"That we will need to be just as circumspect about. I will take it tomorrow and do some research. See if I can find out anything about it. The rest can wait until we're out on the digs."

"You're the man with the plan, Chrissy," he said, bending to lick beads of sweat from my skin. "I'll just follow orders."

I stared at him askance. "Would that it were true," I said. "But I have a feeling I know better."

7

———

As it was, it was nearly three days before I managed to see Lawless again, and even then I had not had time to research anything at all. Royale had kept me very busy indeed, running about and setting up the dig. I had spent one entire day meeting with the headman for our site, laying out the plans and boundaries, talking about the sort of men we needed to hire. Local men were always risky, as some of the best tomb robbers there were came from that stock, and yet they were the cheapest labor.

In the end we hired a good mix of locals and Europeans, got the dig marked off, and set up the visiting area between our site and Zavigny's. It was not until we laid in provisions that I found an excuse to seek out Eric.

"Your men say you have ordered whiskey. I thought I told you that was unwise," I said when I found him, laboring under erecting a tent for his employer.

"Hey, didn't neither me or Zaffiggy order any. Talk to the headman, you got a problem." He wiped sweat from his eyes and peered at me while I tried to ignore the fact that he had stripped to the waist to work, his torso shining in the sun.

His nipples looked bruised, even days after our last encounter.

At least, I hoped it was from our encounter.

"I shall."

He looked me over closely. "You get any research done on the map and all?"

"Not yet, no."

"Well, see if you can't sneak out tonight. We need to get a move on."

A thrill passed through me, thinking that it might just be me he was so impatient to see again and not our map.

"I will try. The valley is fairly accessible by moonlight, so we might just have a chance at that."

"Good. Look, I'll talk to the headman about the whiskey. You get on back to old Royale and get your work done. That way you'll have tonight free." The look he gave me left me no doubt that it was me he wanted to see.

My pulse speeded. "Yes. I shall do that."

The rest of the day passed with agonizing slowness. I worked during the rest of the morning, sweating alongside our diggers to make Royale's tent up, shaking my head over the expensive rugs and the damned mirror I hung from the main pole. The silver flatware would disappear in no time.

During the hottest part of the day, we slept or rested, many of the workers sitting about under the shade tents we had erected and smoking, talking, and laughing.

Supper seemed to take forever, the stringy chicken and unmentionable vegetables making me long for the hotel. It was always the way, I knew. By the second week, I would forget what real food tasted like.

The moon finally rose and Royale declared a good day's work, settling in with his bottle of rotgut to sleep in his chair.

Summarily dismissed, I went to my own tent and dug into the little hole I'd created out of a large flat rock and a few pieces of timber. The map case was there, and I brought it out, not lighting the lantern, as I had no wish for anyone to see my shadow and know what I was about.

I crept away like a thief in the night and met Lawless halfway between our digs, neither of us speaking much until we were well away from the camps.

Then Lawless piped up. "So where are we going?"

"It's quite a stroll," I replied but pointed out the route, nonetheless. "We go there."

"Well, let's get a move on, then."

To his credit, Lawless made the trek easily, the cold night air not affecting him at all. It was most pleasant to walk with him, mostly silent, only the occasional direction necessary. Luckily we were digging in the extreme East Valley, where few tombs had been found, and the walk was not as long as it could have been.

"So is this where we haul out your map?" he asked finally.

"I suppose." Now that we were looking down upon the valley from the cliffs above, the moonlight making it appear alien and intimidating, I was not at all sure that was where we should be, or that we should chance opening the map and distracting ourselves. I somehow found myself looking around, wondering who might be watching, for I swear I felt eyes upon me.

"You sound thrilled, Chrissy. What, you not wanting to share with me?"

Was that his hand on my buttocks? Gracious, but he was familiar.

I removed his hand and gave him an arch look that was

most likely lost on him in the dark. "Here. Give me some light."

We were far enough away from everything that we should be safe lighting a lantern, and Lawless did just that, the tiny flame giving me just enough light to see the map. Gracious, but the map covered a large area, and many of the symbols I simply could not read, the strange language mixed in with the glyphs and hieratic making my eyes hurt.

"Do we even know what we're looking for?" Lawless asked, peering over my shoulder. "I mean, what the map is for?"

The way he said *fer* instead of *for* had me biting my lip to hold in a smile. "Well, one assumes the fellow who gave us this wanted us to find something, and there are several cartouches placed about that would lead me to believe perhaps they are tombs. Still, much of the map is just not translatable."

He crowded closer, rubbing up against me in a most improper way. I sighed and took a step forward. Lawless followed.

"Really," I said, "if we are to play lord and chambermaid, we might have done so without hiking all the way out here."

"Oh, all right. You sure are a killjoy, Chrissy." Lawless dutifully moved away from me, though, and held the lantern a little higher. "Can you at least tell where we are?"

"I would say we're roughly here," I replied, putting a finger to the map where it showed our position on the high edge of the cliff. "The nearest cartouche is here, which is a bit of a hike again."

"Well, if we're gonna lose sleep, I'd rather do it some other way."

I turned to look at him, only to find his face very close to mine, the lantern casting an eerie glow on his eyes.

"Oh, well, yes...."

"Maybe we ought to come back on our rest day, when we have a whole day," Lawless said, his breath brushing against my mouth, warm and scented with whiskey from his supper, I would imagine. "We've got other fish we could fry now."

"Is that all you think about?" My own flirtatious tone surprised me, for I had meant to take on something much more censorious.

"No. But it's what I think about the most when you're around. See?"

In a move as neat as could be, Lawless used the hand not holding the lantern to grab the hand I did not hold the map in and then drew it to the fly of his trousers, holding my hand firmly over the warm bulge there. My eyes flew back to meet his, my mouth falling open, but he simply smiled and moved against my hand, thrusting slowly.

"Feels good, Chrissy."

"Stop calling me that." Again, my words held no heat. How could they when my fingers had gone exploring, cupping him and testing his length and girth?

"What should I call you, then? Darlin'? Sweetheart?" His voice went low, the mocking note leaving it. "Lover?"

"Lover...." Fascinated in spite of myself by the way his hips began to move in short, sharp pulses, I nodded. "I like that."

His hand clenched over mine, pulling it harder against him. "Uh-huh. Me too."

Who knows how long we might have stayed like that, my hand on him, our breath speeding, and our hearts pounding in time? Who indeed? We got no chance to find out, because one moment I was fondling Lawless enthusiastically, and the next I was upon my arse in the dirt and he was standing with his pistol in hand, smoke curling gray in the black night, the shot he'd squeezed off still ringing around the canyon like a crazed bell in an abandoned church.

"What in the name of all holy hell—" I began, only to stop when he pointed.

"Cobra snake," he said, and when I followed the direction of his finger, I saw that he was absolutely right. A dead cobra lay nearly where my feet had been, its flat head severed neatly where it met the caped neck.

Bile rose in my throat. "I... thank you. That could have been very nasty."

"Uh-huh. You know," Lawless said, tilting his head and contemplating the snake, "the bossman showed me all sorts of pictures of these varmints, but in all his time I been here, I ain't seen one. Now, do you reckon us seeing one tonight is coincidence?"

I stared. "What else could it be?"

"I dunno. But it pays to be safe. This whole thing with the map and all...." Lawless shrugged. "Come on and let's git before anyone decides to investigate that shot."

"Yes, yes, of course. A good idea."

We wended our way back toward our camps, and I confess my heart was still racing, my stomach still queasy. I knew the dangers inherent in this desert, but I had rarely come so close to one as I had tonight.

"Well," Lawless said after what seemed like endless trudging, "I set my tent up a ways from the other on the idea that I would guard the entrance to the camp. You're welcome to come with me. We could have a belt."

"Oh." Logic told me to say no, but the rest of me agreed wholeheartedly to a stiff drink. "That would be fine."

I followed him to his tent, placing my feet quietly, though I was not as stealthy as he was. When we got inside, he set aside the dark lantern and I dropped the map, and he was on me like a cat pouncing a mouse, kissing me fiercely. So much so that I tasted blood, in fact, my lip splitting under the pressure.

Kissing back just as hard, I threw my arms about him, holding him to me, feeling the heavy sturdiness of his body and loving how it made me feel ridiculously safe. Nothing could keep me completely safe, and normally I did not even long for it, but in this case, I wanted to feel as if the only thing that could touch me was him.

Fumbling, I reached for the buttons on his shirt, looking for his fine, hot skin. Lawless helped me, stripping bare as a newborn in mere seconds. I ran my hands over his shoulders, down his arms, and then his chest and ribs. My fingertips rubbed over his nipples, and I stopped there when he moaned, pinching them between thumbs and forefingers.

Lawless arched against me, prick hard and bare against my still-clothed belly. "Damn, lover. Again."

"You'd best not call me that too much, or you will pop out with it at a most... oh. There. A most inappropriate time."

His hand had slid between my legs, cupping my privates, and all I could do was hang there, kneeling at his touch and holding on to him when he bent to kiss me again.

"Shut up, lover," he murmured against my mouth, and I did, for his tongue pushed between my lips and no more words could come out.

When he pushed me down on my back on his pallet, I did not fight him, letting him pull off my boots and trousers, my underclothes and my shirt. He looked at me in the canvas-filtered moonlight for long moments before touching me, starting at my throat and working down over my chest.

My own nipples tightened almost painfully when he

pinched them, and when he bent to set his mouth to them, I gasped, squirming on the rough blanket beneath me.

"Like that, huh?" The rasp of his breath, his words, was almost unbearable, and I stifled a cry, on fire for him. I nodded, needing more, and he gave it.

The very tip of his tongue touched my left nipple, pushing it this way and that, and while his mouth played there, his hand found its way between my thighs once more, this time with no cloth to block him. My sacs received the most incredible caress, so soft and sure that I thought I might die to get more of it, firmer, harder.

I pressed myself down, trying to increase the sensation, but Lawless only laughed and grabbed my swinging cock instead, stroking it once, twice, the touch far rougher than the one he had used on my balls.

My sharp bark of pleasure shocked me, and I clapped a hand over my mouth. His triumphant little smile made me want to slap him, but I settled instead for reaching out, trailing my hand over the hairs that laced his belly, then digging them into the much heavier shock of hair about the base of his cock. His groan pleased me to no end. Two of us could play this game.

For long moments we had a standoff, both of us touching and stroking the other, neither of us willing to be the first one to move on. Then Lawless cursed and shifted to lie beside me, bringing me to him for another kiss, then another, until my lips felt swollen, almost burning.

"Want you, Christian."

The use of my full name told me more than anything of his need, and I smiled, kissing his chin and cheeks. "How?" I asked. "How do you want me?"

"I don't... your mouth. Your hands. Whatever I can have."

His hot cheek against mine betrayed that he had other thoughts, as did the way his heart raced. "Oh, I think you might have rather more than that."

While he had seemed experienced enough, I thought perhaps Lawless had partaken little enough of the Greek love that I need not worry about odd ailments. Besides, he had been in my mouth long enough previously, so I sat up, putting one hand to his mouth.

"Suck," I said, dipping two fingers to run along his lower lip.

Drawing in a breath so deep it rocked me where I leaned on his chest, Lawless did just so, licking and sucking at my fingers, getting them wet in the extreme. That would do nicely, and when I pulled them free and reached down between my own legs, his groan fairly shook the tent.

"Do you wish to wake the whole camp?"

"No. But Jesus God, lover...." He stared at me while I pushed my own fingers between my buttocks, flinching a bit at the tightness I found there.

Oh yes, it had been some time since I had given myself this way. Finally I managed to get them in, however, and I readied myself quickly, listening to his harsh breathing and my own pounding heart.

"Get...." I paused, drawing breath. "Get yourself ready, Eric."

His brows lowered. "How?"

"Your hand. Get it wet so you can get yourself slick for me."

At his still-baffled look, I sighed. "Come here," I said, tugging at his thigh with my free hand.

Lawless came readily, his prick slipping right up toward my face. I licked him as if he were an Italian ice, getting his cock good and wet. Then I pushed him back and removed my fingers from my aching arse, spreading my thighs wide.

"Now, if you please."

"Pushy bastard," he said but was quick to set the tip of his cock at my entrance, staring down at me with what looked to be amazement in his expression. "Are you sure?"

I wrapped my legs around his hips and pulled. "Very sure. I need to feel you. Need to feel...."

My words might have trailed off, but he knew, for he nodded. "Alive."

"Yes. Please."

When he began to push inside me, I had to stifle a cry. He stretched me so wide, so incredibly wide, that I thought I might burst. My cock flagged, my whole body straining to fight him off, but I made myself draw breath after deep breath, and finally he was inside me completely, hips seated against my arse.

We stayed just like that for long moments, sweat running on our skin, hot droplets from his chest falling on my belly. Then he began to move, as if he could no longer remain still, his hips moving in tiny, sharp jerks.

I have no notion of when discomfort faded and pleasure took hold, but soon enough my cock hardened once more, slapping my belly as he thrust inside me, and Lawless grunted, one hand closing about me, pulling as he took me.

He was hardly more than a dark shadow above me, and I could have fantasized about him being anyone—a pharaoh, perhaps, or a high priest. Had he done this on our first night together, I might have. Now I only wished I could see his face more clearly.

Reaching up, I touched his chin, the bristles of his beard scratching me, the distinct shape of his lower lip curving along my thumb. We rocked that way for a long time, his prick in me, his hand on my cock, his shocked words falling right into my hand.

Then he moved just slightly, changing the angle of his thrusts, and sparks lit inside me, sliding right up my spine. My body squeezed around him, and suddenly the slow, careful movements he'd made became a frenzy. He thrust into me like there was no tomorrow, and I took everything he gave me gleefully, crossing my ankles at the small of his back and begging for more.

My hand scrabbled at his shoulders, trying to find some purchase in my shifting world as his body rocked into mine, his cock pushing me off-balance over and over. There was none to be found. Lawless was the only solid thing left to me, and he moved inside me like a madman, driving me higher and higher until I soared.

His touch finally pushed me over the edge, his thumb pressing into the exposed slit at the head of my cock, his prick hitting that spot deep inside, and I spent myself, great spurts of come coating my belly and chest as I shot between us.

Deep in my body, Lawless throbbed and shuddered, his prick pushing in one last time before he came. I counted every pulse, listening to his harsh grunts, his animal sounds with a kind of blind joy.

We collapsed together, my body relaxing so profoundly after the tension from our close call with the snake and our lovemaking left me that I hardly felt the rocks digging into my back through his pallet when his weight fell on me.

I did know they were there, however, as a particularly sharp one stuck right into the small of my back.

Stroking Eric's hair, I stared up at the top of the tent, not really seeing it.

Finally he lifted his head and kissed my mouth. "You're not gonna stay, are you?"

"It would be unwise, no doubt," I agreed. "I imagine we've already created fodder for gossip."

"Yeah, well, let 'em talk."

I smiled. Brave talk was all good and well, but men had simply disappeared into the desert for less than what we had just done.

"I should go back to my camp."

"I'll go with you," he said, pulling out of me with a genuinely disappointed sound.

"No need." I fumbled back into my clothes and scooped up the map case.

"Bullshit. I'm the one with the gun."

"Ah, the American cowboy. Very well. You may see me home."

We would have to wait until our rest day to explore further, but I felt we had made some sort of progress that night.

And the rest we had accomplished I would feel for several days afterward.

8

———————

The dig went on as one might expect. Despite Royale's disappointment that we had not discovered the next big tomb, we had unearthed some marvelous pottery shards and ushabtis. Whether my employer knew it or not, that meant we had found burial leavings. Admittedly they could have been leftovers from ancient tomb robbers.

They could have been trash heaps as well. Oh, I thought that would have been wonderful, to find a site where the priests had done their burial work.

I did not see Lawless for nearly a week, and it chafed on me. As if he knew I needed to be away, Royale kept me hopping, running this way and that. Every day I had to explain the rest period to him as well. The fact was that no one could work in the middle of the day, including Royale, but he felt he was not getting his money's worth.

The men were restless from it, and we all breathed a sigh of relief when the first day off rolled about. I got Royale settled with all of the news and correspondence that had come in the previous day, and off I went, my hat on my head, the map case in my hand.

"He is in the tent with the effendi," one of Zavigny's workers said when I questioned him about Lawless, and I sighed, nodding. The men were all smoking, so I moved away under a smaller tarp that had been set up near the worksite and sat, thinking on all the things I needed to get done. Waiting.

I must have dozed. When I woke, it was not to Lawless shaking me awake. The hand on my shoulder belonged to a thin Egyptian man wrapped in a black robe that covered all but his eyes.

Surely I had cause to jump, and the squeak that left me was less than manly, but there you are. I blinked at him, cringing back a bit.

"Find the king," he said in heavily accented English. "Release him."

"Th-the king?" I stammered. "What king?"

"Find the king," he repeated and seemed to shimmer, dissolving into nothing more than a fine black dust, carried away on the slight breeze.

Lawless appeared, walking through the remains of the man like there had been nothing there.

"Well, hey there, Chrissy."

"Would you stop calling me that!" Jumping to my feet, I brushed off my trousers. "Did you not see that?"

"See what?" His gray eyes glinted in the late day sun, his smile white and bright. I wanted to smack him.

"That man. The man who disintegrated."

"You musta been dreaming, Chr.... Lover. I swear, wasn't nothing there."

"There was indeed. He said to find the king. To free him."

"That was a helluva dream." Lawless shook his head. "It's damned hot, but I'm ready to tramp about if you are."

There was no point arguing that it had not been a dream, for I could see despite what had happened to us before with the mysterious clawed man and the snake, he was not concerned.

"Did you bring your water?" I insisted we both carry water containers. Who knew what could happen?

"You blind as well as dreamstruck?" he asked, thumping a canteen that hung from his shoulder. "Come on."

"Yes, yes." Out of sorts, I tromped along after him, trying to ignore the way the men watched us go. Their whispers seemed more inquisitive than not, so I let them pass, knowing if I looked guilty or got upset, that would turn them to downright speculation.

We were dripping sweat and panting by the time we reached the West Valley and I wondered, not for the first time, if I had lost my mind. What was I doing, out in the hottest part of the day, tromping about looking for some tomb that most likely had never existed, pointed to it by a freak and accompanied by a brash American gunslinger?

Clearly I had taken leave of my senses.

"You're supposed to be reading the map, Chrissy, not thinking. You think too much."

I vow, I had no control over my body when I turned and landed a wild, swinging blow to his cheek.

"Stop calling me that!" I shouted, the sound echoing crazily off the canyon walls.

His head had snapped back with the blow, and his hand went to his cheek, but Lawless grinned at me all the same. "If you wanted to get naked, we should have stayed at camp," he said.

"I—You—How on earth...?" I took a deep breath and

pulled myself together, my tone icy when I went on. "I cannot imagine how you could equate my hitting you with wanting to do... that."

"Because you're too damned attractive in a rage, Chrissy. Now where are we?"

"I am in Hades. You, I have no idea. You live in the tiny locked room that is your own mind."

"God, I love it when you get huffy." He still smiled at me like the village idiot.

I sighed. "We are roughly here," I said, consulting the map. "We need to go here."

The point that it was much easier to see landscape features in the day only mollified me a tiny bit. I began marching along, muttering about the map and how someone might have updated it with new features if they were going to be so kind as to make a reproduction for us.

Which is why I almost missed seeing Eric fall, only his sharp cry alerting me soon enough to see where he went off the trail.

"Eric!" I shouted that, as well I am ashamed to say, as many other things, some endearments, some curses. Scrambling to the edge of the trail where it turned back sharply on itself, I peered over, attempting to avoid sending any more earth sliding down atop him.

"Right here, lover. Twisted up a little, though. Can you give me a hand?"

Indeed, he had not fallen far, a ledge below having caught his drop. Still, I could see that one leg was twisted under him, and that if he moved without something to stabilize him, he might fall.

I cast about desperately for something to pass down for him to grab on to and found nothing useful. In the end it was my canteen, the sturdy canvas strap just long enough to reach.

"Grab on," I said. "I shall try to help you up."

His weight nearly numbed my hand when he latched on, but between me pulling and him pushing, we got him back on the rather narrow trail, and I supported him while he limped to a wider patch on the path.

"You should let me look at that ankle," I said, watching him wince with every step.

"If I take off my boot now, I won't never get it back on," he argued, and he had a point. "You got anything I can tie it up with a little?"

We had traveled rather lightly, and again, my canteen became the savior. I unhooked the strap from the bottle and handed it to him so he might wrap it around his boot for extra support.

"Well. Now what?" he asked.

"Now we go back to camp. We cannot risk injuring you further."

His face took on a very stubborn cast. "We got to keep going, lover. We're never going to find it at this rate. Hell, today might be our last chance for a bit."

Both digs were reaching the state where Lawless and I might be needed even on rest days, so I knew he had a point. I also knew I was strangely reluctant to risk him.

"It has been here for thousands of years, whatever it is. It can wait another season if need be, and we have the map." Ducking, I set my shoulder under his arm and hauled him upright. "Now, come along."

"Yeah, yeah. All right. Just watch the path."

"I will. What happened, anyway?"

He shrugged, his rolling shoulders nearly sending us

staggering again. "I dunno. One minute it was solid rock under my feet. The next I swear it felt like quicksand."

"How very odd."

"Yeah, well, this whole thing is odd," he said, rolling his eyes at me. "From one to another, each time we do something on this, it gets worse."

"You told me today I was imagining things. I think perhaps it's your turn." Really, if he could dismiss my encounter with the robed man, I could do the same for his falling sands.

"Uh-huh. I don't believe in magic and shit. But I do believe in booby traps. Someone out to get you, lover? Someone I don't know about?"

"I shouldn't think so." I had no enemies in Egypt, at least not that I knew of. "Perhaps someone has it in for you."

"Nah. I'm not the one seeing shit when you're not around. You're doing it when I'm not, though."

Bugger. Well, that would be just my luck, to have someone playing a game with me. But who? I would put my mind to it that night, when I was not under the scorching Egyptian sun, helping to carry a man who seemed to weigh twice the stone he had earlier in the day.

"I need some water."

It took us twice as long to return as it had to venture out, and by the time we got back to Zavigny's camp, we were both soaked to the skin with sweat and rubbed raw from him leaning on me and giving the insidious grit that clung to us places to rub.

"Old Zaffiggy has set up a bath station of sorts, if you wanna get clean," Lawless said, the lines around his mouth and eyes deep and white. It made his suggestion seem even more selfless, and it went a long way toward putting me back in charity with him.

"Thank you, but I think we should look at your ankle first."

"What has happened? Eric! You have had an injury?"

Oh, what rotten luck, I thought. Lawless agreed, for he let out a soft curse. It was Zavigny, trotting right over to us and tutting.

"What has happened?" he asked, staring at us one to another.

"We were out making a survey of the north corner," I said quickly, before Lawless could say whatever he had drawn breath to say. "The sand hid a large crevasse, and Mr. Lawless twisted his ankle."

Luckily the map case and the map were tucked neatly in my expedition bag, out of sight.

"La, we must see to that, then. I need you on your feet and ready to go tomorrow, Eric."

"I'll be fine, sir. Christian was about to help me out." Those gray eyes danced when Lawless said my full name, telling me how easy it would have been to call me Chrissy, or worse, lover.

"Indeed," I agreed. "If you could just send someone with salve and bandages, we can manage quite well on our own."

"No, no. I will help. And then you must come to my tent for a drink, Christian. I have something I want to show you."

I looked at Lawless, who raised his brows and shrugged. He obviously had no idea what the good doctor wished to show me.

"Very well."

Lawless's ankle was not as badly injured as I feared, and Zavigny proved remarkably helpful. He bandaged the sprain after I spread it with a stinky salve, and then he insisted Lawless have a lie-down to recover from his trauma.

"But you said you had something...."

"To show Christian, which I do. You have not the training I need for this, Eric."

For all of his earlier kindness, the tone Zavigny used then was one of employer to staff, and while I could see it put Eric's back up, he obeyed, shrugging and limping off to sit with the men. My last view of him had him begging a smoke off someone, rolling tobacco in a bit of paper.

"I'm not sure I can be of any assistance," I told Zavigny when we entered his tent. "You are far more experienced than I."

"Yes, but this is something quite odd." Rummaging through a large piece of cheesecloth, Zavigny brought out what looked like a painted statuette at first glance, something stylized, rather like the statues and paintings of the Pharaoh Akhenaten, who was Nefertiti's husband, and not known for his presence in the Valley of Kings.

On closer inspection, however, it became clear that while the stone was very similar, as well as the almost female roundness of the body, that was where the similarity ended. The head on the statuette was not human, nor was it one of the usual animal representations common in Egyptian mythology. It seemed so misshapen as to be broken, I thought, but the edges were far too clean for that.

Atop the neck sat a long, curling tentacle, almost like the tongue of a bird, only it contained spikes at the end. The other anomaly was the hands. Instead of the usual flat, human hands, the statue had claws, hugely disproportionate to body.

"Where did you get this?" I asked, studying the grotesque little thing. It stood only about nine inches tall, but it seemed much larger and surprisingly cold in my hand.

"At this grid here," Zavigny replied, pointing out a plot

near where his dig met Royale's. "I wanted to ask if you had seen anyone, or if your men had reported anyone who might be planting artifacts."

"Well, why would someone plant something such as this? If one wanted a find to be believed, they would be more careful to follow the symbology."

"Yes, I thought that too, but it never hurts to ask."

"I suppose. I shall ask the headman."

"Thank you. What do you make of it?"

"A sculptor's flight of fancy, perhaps? It seems authentic enough in age. Did you notice how cold it is?"

"I did. At first I thought obsidian, perhaps trade goods, but the stone does not have that high gloss."

"No, it is much more a dull surface."

I snuck a glance at the Frenchman's face. He appeared tired, his wrinkles showing in great quantities. His mouth was tight as well. Something about the freakish little thing bothered him deeply. I could not blame him. It was rather obscene.

"I would say it's not trade goods, though. Look at the style, the construction. It's classic to this area."

"It is." Zavigny sighed again, and I peered at him, leaving off the covert stares. He met my eyes. "I admit, I knew this dig was unusual, but I was truly hoping for something...." He trailed off, his mouth a thin line.

"I confess, Professor, I had wondered why you chose here, so far from the rest of the action. On my employer's part that is natural, as he failed to file his plan early enough and is not well known in the field. You, though, could have been closer to Carter."

"There is an untapped mine of artifact here, *mon ami*. Last season a grave robber brought me this."

Going to his trunk, he pulled out and unwrapped a

small golden statue of the type that had sent people into spasms after the opening of Tutankhamen's tomb. The shape was not of any human king, though. It was that of Osiris, the king god of the ancients and the ruler of the underworld.

My eyes fairly bugged out, I am sure, for while I was accustomed to seeing such things in museums, I confess that seeing one handled so casually was unusual.

"Are you sure it's from this grid?"

"The, er, provenance is fairly certain. I feel that between here and the West Valley, we will find a great deal of untapped territory."

Only a few weeks ago I would have scoffed at the idea, as no one else had ever formed any such theory. Now I thought he might just be right.

"Well, sir. I mean no offense, but why tell me all of this? I work for the competition, so to speak."

"Bah. Royale is a fool. I tell you this because I know you are a true digger, *mon ami*. Eric is a fine guard and an intelligent man, but he is no archaeologist. I will need your help to classify and catalog things, and you will need my help if Royale finds anything worthwhile, to keep him from selling it to the highest bidder."

Ah. Certainly true, and very uplifting to me at the time, as I was feeling the worst sort of hired hand. So much so that I impulsively offered my services.

"I shall help in any way I can, sir."

"Excellent." He clapped me on the shoulder with his free hand. "You may start by investigating the area where I found this."

Not the gold. The dark stone monster. Naturally. He carefully wrapped up Osiris and handed me the strange little tentacle figure.

"Eric is at your disposal. All is not safe."

Something in his tone had me staring at him again, and his face still held that cast of a man who was tired and wary. I would swear fear flashed in his eyes.

"Have you seen him?" I asked, quite appalled that I had blurted it out.

I need not have worried, for he only nodded. "I have. Be careful. Now go on, lad. I'm sure you have things to do."

"Thank you, sir."

"Oh, wait." With another turn to his trunk, he tossed me a little bag, one that jingled with coin. "Expense money. I know that Royale comes first, but I would not have you work for me with no recompense."

I stared at the little bag for a long moment before nodding and tucking it away in my bag where the map case seemed to be burning a hole. "Thank you, sir."

Thus dismissed, I left. I had a great deal to think about.

9

Lawless hailed me when I left Zavigny's tent, waving at me from where he sat in the shade, his ankle propped up on a crate. I walked over to him, my nose wrinkling at the smell of the salve the professor had used.

"Yeah, I know. Powerful stuff in this heat, I tell you. What did he want to show you?"

"Some items from the dig," I answered, glancing about. "I promise to let you in later, but now is not the time."

"Long as you're not holding out on me, Chrissy."

"How's your face?" I rejoined, pointing to his cheek.

That got me a deep laugh, merry as could be. "Better than my ankle. You're a vicious little bastard, though, I have to give you that. You can hold your own better than I thought."

"It has served me well." If only I had known how well I would need it to serve me in the future I might not have been so proud of myself. "I do wish you would cease calling me that ridiculous diminutive, though."

"Was that English?" He winked at me, gray eyes sparkling. "When do you want to meet?"

"It can wait until the next rest day." Holding up a hand when he would have protested, I went on. "We have aroused enough suspicion, and I have a feeling that we no longer need to dance around your employer, at least. So he will let you go when I send for you. Besides, your ankle needs a few days to heal, if you insist upon flinging yourself off cliffs."

"I told you, it just let go."

"And I say it felt solid enough to me when I was pulling you up." Suddenly exhausted, I rolled my shoulders and head. "I am going back to spend the rest of the rest day... well, resting. I'll let you know when I am ready to engage the battle again."

"Uh-huh. As long as I get something really good for waiting, I'll be fine." There was no mistaking the lascivious look in his eye, and I flushed hot with something other than sunburn.

"I am sure we can work something out."

"Oh, good. See you later," he said. "Lover."

That word followed me all the way back to camp, where I went to my tent and took out my writing box, handily avoiding Royale's tent. I needed to record the events that had occurred, as well as the grid where the statue had been found, before I forgot.

Then the heat got to me at last, and I succumbed to the need for a nap, curling up on my pallet and dozing off, my thoughts torn between the map, Zavigny's artifacts, and some erotic notions of what I could reward Lawless with.

10

_____

The throne was hewn of a single block of black stone, painted with gold glyphs on plaster. The king sat with his hands flat on the arms of the throne, facing forward, his eyes blank and his face unmoving.

Next to the king stood a dark-skinned man, slender and small, whose eyes appeared like bottomless pools of oil. He whispered in the king's ear, hand waving languidly at the mass of petitioners that knelt before the throne. A smile played across his face, wide and white.

The king nodded once, as though a man in a dream, and the magician-priest clapped his hands in delight before raising his arms and chanting, an invocation of sorts that got louder and louder until the whole room rang with it, making the waiting subjects quail.

The very walls shook, and a dark cloud, one that shifted like the mist of some unspeakable evil, appeared over the heads of the front row of petitioners. Out of the mist appeared a serpent-like creature, its long, ropy body undulating, its wings like those of a bat, leathery and huge.

It filled the air above the throne, its very skin writhing and *changing, as if it was composed of a nest of snakes, and the people below screamed in horror when it swooped down among them. Its tail wrapped about three men and lifted them up off the floor, screaming as the serpent fed them into its mouth, one after the other. The sound of bones wrenching and grinding to dust ricocheted crazily about the chamber.*

The magician laughed, maniacal and alien above the screams of the next three people consumed.

The king never moved.

I woke up for the third night in a row to just that dream, gasping, sweat running on my skin.

There was no such serpent in the Egyptian mythos, I felt certain. Most of the snake deities and symbols were based on the cobra. So why was I dreaming about the man I had seen that day while waiting for Lawless, summoning a monster that must be a figment of my imagination?

I was not a man given to fancies.

Rising, I made short work of my ablutions, intending to ask Royale for a bit of time off. When I left my tent, however, I was accosted by the foreman of our dig. Silad Mujallah had been most excellent, needing very little direction, which was good, as I usually had to deal with our employer so the men could work.

This morning he seemed agitated. "Sayyid! You must come," he said, reaching out to tug at my arm.

Egyptians were much more physical with one another than the British, but usually they deferred to my custom and left me be, so whatever he wanted me to see must be important.

Following him down the path to the dig, I found the men gathered in a tight knot around a small pit, talking excitedly. Royale was there, his booming voice rising above the others.

"Christian! Ah, there you are, boy. Come and look! Told you we would find something worthwhile!"

"What is it?" I climbed down into the pit, the men parting ranks and then closing behind me. The smell of unwashed bodies momentarily blinded me, my eyes watering. When they cleared, however, I could see what Royale was waving under my nose.

"That looks like a piece of canopic jar," I said, searching out Silad's gaze. He nodded at me, grinning wide and white.

"Well, of course it does. That's what it is, isn't it?" Royale nearly danced in his excitement.

I, on the other hand, felt a cold chill. "That's an odd thing to find in wash down or midden."

"What are you saying?" Royale demanded, hushing the murmur that went through the men. "You think this shouldn't be here, boy?"

It would not do to raise suspicion among the men, so I merely smiled. "Not at all. If there is one thing I have learned about Egypt, it is to expect the unexpected."

I held out a hand, hoping my imperious gesture would have him putting the jar in my grasp. It did indeed, Royale handing it over with an almost bemused look. His face was red in the extreme, and I smiled kindly at him.

"Silad and I will catalog this. Once we've finished with all the information we need, I shall join you at your tent to look it over more closely."

Royale looked about at the ring of nodding men and gave in rather more easily than I thought he would. "Just be quick about it," he muttered and stomped off, roaring as the men got in his way.

I slanted a glance at Silad, who let out a positive flurry of Arabic, sending the men scrambling back to work. Then he joined me.

"You think it was, how you say? Planted?" he asked, his dark eyes bright and keen.

"I'm not sure. One way or the other, your crew will get credit for it, Silad. Well done."

"*Shukran*, sayyid. I will tell them. They will be pleased."

"Good, good. Now show me where you found it exactly. And recommend two honest men to guard the site tonight."

Once something of value had been found, the thieves would descend like flies on a donkey pile. I would have to speak to Royale about hiring a couple of Americans or Europeans to stand guard from now on. The men of the local villages were not bad men, but thieving was in their blood, and they saw it as no more than reclaiming something that was their birthright.

Silad, however, had been educated by the best Egyptian in the business and believed that only by putting artifacts in museums could he save his heritage.

So he nodded at me, grinning a little with shared pride. "I have picked the men already. Here is where we found it. I had the little German man sketch it."

One of the Europeans Royale had hired on turned out to be an excellent artist. Much better, in fact, than he was at digging. At that he proved rather clumsy.

We marked off the piece on the map, and I wondered once more how such expensive grave goods were just lying about. Not just our jar, but Zavigny's statuettes. It was as if someone were laying a trail of crumbs for us, as if the dig season were some demented Egyptian fairy tale.

When I took the jar to Royale, he beamed proudly, showing me the box he had already had made to ship it in.

"It'll look fine, won't it, boy?"

"In the museum? Oh yes."

His face took on a thunderous cast. "No, in my house, my

lad. This is far too fine to sit on a dusty museum shelf and fade away."

The jar was splendid; there was no doubt of that. Even uncleaned, the fine ivory was clear, the detail work of the scrolled head which served as a lid small and perfect. One whole side appeared to be missing, and thus the contents were gone, but really it was an excellent specimen.

"What do you think the head was supposed to be?" he asked. "Aren't they usually Horus or something?"

"The sons of Horus, actually. They were generally represented as a man, a falcon, a baboon, and a dog. Some burials have all human heads, of course, but this one appears almost reptilian."

"You mean like a snake?" His great girth pressed against my side when he bent to look, and I pulled away a bit.

"Not a cobra, no. But perhaps a great lizard or serpent, nonetheless."

"Huh. Well, one way or the other, I intend to have it."

Grimacing, I handed it over. "As you say. I think we should give the men the rest of the day off, sir."

"Why on earth would I do that?" he boomed. "We'll lose momentum."

"Pardon my saying so, sir, but you'll lose more than momentum if you keep on digging today. Better to tell the men that they're getting a half of a day for such an excellent find and setting guards on the site. That way, Silad can explore and make sure nothing else of importance is in that grid."

"Before it disappears, you mean?" At my nod, he clapped me on the shoulder. "Good idea. Yes, yes, you'll tell Silad for me, hmm? I want to admire my jar."

I feared it would be worse than Royale simply taking the thing for himself. No, I imagined he would sell it to a collector friend, and that beautiful piece of the past would be locked away forever from sight of the public.

Sighing, I turned away and made my way back down to the dig, where a great cheer went up upon my announcement of the rest day. Silad only laughed and called me the so-smart sayyid, waving the men off and telling them to go and smoke and *fahddle* and leave him be.

"You have your guards?" I asked before I left him.

"Yes, sayyid. No worry."

I only wished it would be that easy. But between my dreams and the strange goings-on, I felt I had much to worry about.

11

———

Dusk threatened by the time I made my way to Zavigny's camp that night, and the professor himself greeted me with a smile.

"Ah! Christian! I hear you have made a find."

"Silad Mujallah has made a find," I returned. "He is an excellent headman. Soon he will be out of someone like Royale's reach."

"We all must start somewhere, hmm? Tell me what you have found."

I told him, describing the thing in great detail. "This is the third fine artifact we've found in this area," I finished, "and the second that has a form that deviates from the traditional symbology. What do you think it means, Professor?"

He stroked his little beard, looking pensive. "Perhaps a cult? There were many more than we think, you know. Look at Akhenaten. Look at the widespread cult of Isis, reaching even to Rome."

"Yes, but what kind of cult? I have never seen reference to anything like these creatures."

"Well, then we will have to become reference. Are you

here to take Lawless on a fact-finding mission? He is, how he would say, chomping at the bit to get out and do.”

“No doubt.” I had not seen Lawless for four days, and I admitted to chomping at the bit myself somewhat.

“Well, go on, then. And thank you for keeping me abreast of the find.”

“Quite welcome, sir.”

At least I felt like I had earned some of the coin he had so generously given me.

For his part, Lawless was lurking just outside the professor’s tent, scaring years off my life when he grabbed me and pulled me into the deep shadows that ran between canvas and rock wall.

“Are you trying to make my heart fail?” I demanded, pushing against his chest.

He laughed at me, his eyes the barest dark gleam in the gathering night. “What heart? Whatcha doin’, Chrissy?”

“Updating the professor.”

“Yeah, he says you’re splitting time between camps now. I’m betting old Royale don’t know that, though.”

“You would win that bet. I have not mentioned it, no.”

“Well, then. What are you gonna give me to keep your secret?”

I could not resist playing along. “What would you like?”

“Oh, I think we could start with a kiss, lover.” Without any more warning than that, his hands fell on my shoulders and Lawless kissed me nearly silly, stealing my breath with the strong press of his mouth over mine. Possibly he had missed me as much as I had him. Ridiculous, how attached I had become to him over the short time we had known each other, especially given my initial impression of him.

Without thought, I wrapped my arms about his neck to help hold him where I might deepen the kiss. I moaned into his mouth as his tongue pressed my lips open, pushing in and out in a fine approximation of a more intimate act.

"Shhh," he whispered against my mouth. "The boss might hear."

"Or someone else," I agreed. "Shall we go to your tent, where I may give you the rest of your reward?"

"Hell, yes."

We did not run, hand in hand, as people do in those horrible romances women love so. Lawless could not run with his stiff, though healing, ankle. Instead we went different ways, he to the right, I to the left, to meet inside his tent. I ducked in only seconds before him.

It was enough for me to prepare to meet him, though, and I caught him off guard this time, flinging myself at him to kiss him hard, my hands cupping his cheeks.

"Christian," he moaned, and I could not hide my triumph at the use of my full name.

"What else would you have of me?" I asked. "My mouth? My hands? My body?"

He jerked against me as the whole realm of possibility opened to him, and his cock nudged my hip through the layers of our clothes. His eyes gleamed lighter than the darkness, just enough to give him an utterly wicked cast.

"I want your mouth first, lover."

Yes. He liked that, liked it when I licked and sucked him to completion. I dropped to my knees on the hard ground, covered only by a thin layer of rug, and winced a little as my joints protested. Still, it was no hardship to open his trousers and pull out his cock, running my tongue greedily along the length from base to tip and back again.

"Jesus, lover. Jesus Christ." His hands pulled at my shoulders while I sucked him in, my lips sealed tight around him with no further ado. I felt him tremble, smelled the deep, rich scent of him, and oh, how good he tasted. Salty and bitter and hot as the desert in the day, and I needed more. Immediately.

I sucked at him, working my hands into his trousers to push them down so I could find his balls, working them with the palm of my hand, rolling them gently in their sacs. He went up on tiptoe, his muscles tense as boards, his breath coming in great heaving gasps above me.

Momentarily breaking off from his prick, I ducked to lick at his balls, curving the flat of my tongue around each in turn, scraping it along the skin between. His cry must have alerted someone to what we did, loud as it was. I could only hope a hearer might assume he was with a woman.

"Christian! God, please," he said, much lower than his other noise, his hands in my hair now, guiding me back up.

I did not begrudge him at all, popping my mouth back over the head of his cock, sucking all the way down, my tongue moving along the underside as I went. One more good tug at his balls had him grunting, and when I buried my nose in the blond curls at the base of his cock, he spent for me in great, uncontrolled bursts.

Licking him clean before pulling back, I stroked his thighs, the tiny hairs there catching at my calluses.

"Good?" I asked when he tilted my head up so I might see his face.

"Better than. Want you to... well. Uh...." He trailed off, appearing embarrassed in the extreme, and I admit at first I did not understand him.

"You want me to get you firm once more so I may ride you?"

He shook his head. "No. I want you to... do the doing, lover. Want you to do to me what I been doing to you."

Comprehension dawned. "You want me to fuck you."

"Chrissy!" How scandalized he sounded. "I mean, yeah, but God Almighty, the way you say things."

"Have you any oil? I fear I might hurt you otherwise." Clearly he had not done that with other men, at least not much, for his reactions to the other things we had done had never reached this height of discomfort.

"In my kit bag," he said in a strangled voice. "I use it to.... Well, you know."

I did indeed. What man did not? I have always believed that no matter what the doctors called it, it was not abusive to use one's hand.

The kit bag yielded the oil, as promised, and I set about to relax him and ready him at the same time. "Strip off," I said. "This will go much better if you do."

His hands went to his braces, which hung oddly loose, but then he stopped and stared at me.

"What?" I asked.

"Ain't you gonna get your kit off too?"

My cock throbbed behind my buttons, and I thought it best for my control not to loose it just yet. "Of course I will. But not yet. You test me to my limits, Eric. I fear a stray touch would end things too soon."

Smiling, obviously pleased with that thought, Lawless stripped off his remaining clothing. Then he knelt down in front of me, meeting me on the same level for a scorching kiss.

I gasped into the contact, my muscles jumping under my skin, every nerve in me suddenly firing. I could only turn the tables on him to get him to see what he did to me, and to that end I put my hands over his nipples, feeling them dig into my palms a moment. Then my fingers and thumbs met to squeeze those little bits of flesh, and Lawless groaned for me, his body rolling in a sensuous undulation.

"The things you know how to do," he said, kissing the corner of my mouth. "Do more."

"Of course," I said. Laughing, I took up the oil again and unstoppered it, getting three of my fingers wet on my right hand. I pushed around behind him with my hand, and I gave him two fingers to start, not wanting to hurt, but wanting him to feel it.

His hips rolled, his mouth hanging open and his eyes going wide.

"So much, lover," he said, gasping out each word. "Burns."

"I imagine so," I agreed. "This will help."

Stretching him, preparing him, was the most sexual thing I had ever done. Though still covered in cloth, my cock rubbed at him, battering at my fly like a living creature with a mind of its own. My fingers remained steadier, as I would not hurt him for the world, and when I introduced the third into him, I felt him shake, felt the hardness of his cock rising against me once more.

"Want you naked, Chrissy," he said, tearing at my shirt, and I nodded.

"Yes. Now."

Pulling gently away from his body was no easy task, as his hole sucked at me, squeezed my fingers in a most demanding fashion. I managed it, and yanked at my clothing, tugging it off and tossing it aside, freeing my aching prick in the process.

I used another generous helping of oil on my cock, then returned to him.

"How would you like to do this, Eric?" I asked. "On all fours is easier, but if you wish to watch...."

"I wish. Please."

"On your back, then." I pushed him over to his cot,

easing him down on his back, and crawled up between his legs, placing myself between them. My cock nudged at his tiny, hot hole.

"Ready?"

"Goddamn it, Christian, would you put it in me already?" Eric grabbed my hips and yanked, and I slid in a scant inch, the head slipping into his opening.

His eyes popped wide open, very pale in the dark tent, and I heard his deep groan echo around us.

My own moan sounded loud to my ears when I slid home, the whole length of me buried within him. I had honestly never dreamed that a man like Lawless would allow this, and so had not even begun to contemplate how good it would feel. Had I pondered it, I felt sure at that moment that it would have been a matter of underestimation.

We began to move, his hips pushing up, my cock rubbing inside of him. We rocked together, my hand braced on either side of his chest, his beginning to move upon me as if he had just remembered he had fingers. Lawless touched my cheeks, my throat, his rough hands moving down my chest to pinch at my nipples as I had his, making me gasp and grunt and buck.

It seemed to go on and on, the heat between us enough to warm the cold desert night that had descended, both of us moaning and panting. He was hotter inside than anything I had ever felt, so tight it almost hurt. My balls slapped against his ass, the added layer of sensation practically more than I could bear.

"Eric. Please." I had no idea what I was begging for; I just knew I needed something more.

He reached down to touch himself, his hand closing around his own solid prick, and that made his muscles clench around me, tightening down unmercifully. That was it. That was what I needed.

I added my touch to his, wrapping my fingers about his and pulling hard, so his back bowed off the cot and his body tried to swallow me whole.

My eyes rolled in my head while I pounded into him, my arms shaking as I tried to hold up my weight. He was no help, thrashing under me like his very world might end if he did not arrive soon.

I understood how he felt.

"Now, Eric," I said, pulling hard at his cock, slamming my prick into him over and over. "You must spend for me now."

Much to my amazement, he did just that. His head fell back against the cot, and that strong throat worked when he shot, his come covering the back of my hand and my wrist. Inside he became like a vise, squeezing down on me until I feared that I might simply disappear right into him.

When I spent myself, it was with a violence I had never encountered, my blood rushing in my ears and my muscles trembling from lack of air. My vision blurred, my whole body overheated and shaking, and I filled him as deeply as anyone had ever filled me, giving him all I had to give.

Collapsing upon him when my arms gave out, I lay there panting, wondering if I would ever have the strength to rise.

"How many secrets does that ensure?" I asked when I could breathe again.

He merely laughed, patting my arse and kissing my throat. "A whole mess," he replied. "A whole big old mess."

12

We dozed for some time, but Lawless finally woke me in the dark hours before dawn, reminding me I had to return to my own camp.

"I'll walk with you," he said, assuming his clothes as I put on mine.

"That's ridiculous," I returned. "You have a bad ankle."

"It's mostly healed. And you're the one running around with Zaffiggy's statue in your bag. What in hell did you come to update him on, anyway?"

I turned to stare at him, though it was mostly lost in the darkness, I am sure. "Didn't I tell you? We found an artifact on our site today. One as significant as the statuette of Zavigny's, at least."

"No shit? Well, I tell you, good shit is dropping all over, huh?"

"Yes. Does it strike you as odd?"

"Well, I dunno. You're the expert."

"I thought I was, yes. This is beyond my realm of experience, however."

His hand landed on my back, pulling me to him to give me a warm, wet kiss. "Well, we'll take it as it comes. Come on, Chrissy. Let's get you home."

"Would you stop that?"

"The kissing?"

I nearly trod on his foot hard enough to break it. "The name."

"Yeah, yeah." He steered me out, his confidence in the dark rather more than mine, judging from the way he held me close to his side.

We walked in relative silence, the gap between our camps not nearly enough to allow much in the way of conversation. Not without alerting the guards. We managed to avoid them, as my tent sat nowhere near the site of the finding.

Lawless was only limping a little when we gained my tent, and he stopped me in the shadow of it, where we were highly unlikely to be seen. "This is where I get off," he said. "You watch your back."

Ah. So he did wonder too. I nodded, leaning against him a moment. "You as well. I shall see you soon."

"You'd better."

With another kiss he was gone, fading into the night far more easily than I would have, the sound of his boots echoing on stone the only sound I heard for long moments.

Strangely worried about entering my tent, I went instead to the small kitchen tent, which was already smoking with Fajeed's breakfast fire. There was strong coffee, and at my request, water for tea, which I took out with me while I sat on a flat rock and contemplated the chill in my bones. The cool night could not account for all of it.

13

———

The late morning found me accosted by my employer. I admit, I was bleary enough that I failed to see him coming and so did not steel myself for the encounter.

"Where were you this morning, boy?" he exclaimed. "I am to meet the Director General of Antiquities! I need you to help me dress."

"The Director General?" Surely he had not called in the Bureau of Antiquities for our find, even though that might be protocol. I knew he meant to keep what he dug.

"I got the message not a half hour ago. What the hell is he going to want, I ask you? I swear to God, boy. If any of those fools you hired called them in...."

"I assure you, if they did it was without my word." Though it was entirely possible that Silad Mujallah had, and if he had, I would give him a bonus.

Trailing along behind him, I ignored everything until I heard, "That damned Frenchman...."

"Beg pardon, sir?" I asked.

"I said it had better not be that damned Frenchman. I knew working with him would be a terrible idea."

"He's not so close as to know what we're doing," I argued. "I am sure he did nothing of the kind. You are not without influence, sir. Perhaps he wants to see if you are happy with your permit."

Royale was not well known or well liked, but he had money. A great deal of it. That went a long way with the Director General.

"Bah. Help me get this monkey suit on." He wanted his good suit, not his evening kit, but goodness, he would melt in it. By the time we got him trussed, his florid face had gone a deep red.

"Are you sure you…?"

"Shut it, boy. Is the tie straight?"

"Yes, sir."

"Good. Now go get the cook to make something like little sandwiches or some such. Oh, and Christian?"

"Sir?"

"Keep your mouth shut."

"Of course."

The encounter left me even more out of sorts, and I left the tent, putting my feet down hard. Dust rose under my boots, which gave me a small sense of satisfaction. At least until I nearly ran into the entourage that accompanied the Minister of Antiquities.

"Ah, Christian! There you are. I had heard you were with Royale this season."

Damnation. It was just my luck to run first into Marion Keyes, who was a cousin of my mother's. A round-faced, jovial man with bright rodent eyes, he was very active in Egyptology, and sadly, very nosy.

This did not bode well at all, despite the fact that it was he who had garnered me my first position in Egypt.

"Hello, Marion," I ventured. "What on earth is all of this?"

"This" was a veritable train of camels and donkeys carrying suited men, ladies dressed in riding attire, and photographers lugging their equipment.

"Never fear, my boy," he said, clapping me on the back, his yellowing teeth showing under his little gray beard. "We're merely here for some publicity."

"We don't really need it at the moment, Marion."

His bright brown eyes narrowed, his cheeks scrunching up in a manner that reminded me of nothing so much as an overly intelligent squirrel. "You've found something."

I sighed. What had Royale said? I should have kept my mouth shut. I fobbed it off with a smile. "Nothing but midden and the remains of tomb robbers, but it is enough to make my employer very secretive and worried that the ministry will snatch his goodies."

"Well, you know there's no need to worry on that," he said, poking me with his cane. "We'll just chat, take a few pictures, and head on over to see Zavigny."

Even worse. Still, I tried not to let it show. "Very well. Shall I fetch Royale?"

"Yes, yes, by all means. And we must sit and have tea, you and I, and catch up on family business."

Family business. Oh good God. Without another word I turned on my heel and went to fetch Royale, merely shrugging when he asked me what was what. I knew my attitude annoyed him, but what could I say that would not make matters worse?

"Ah, there you are," Marion said when we arrived. He pumped Royale's hand. "We just wish to have some tea. Let our artists and such wander a bit. I trust that's all right. Here's the Director General."

The Director General was a Frenchman, Pierre Lacau, a distinguished fellow with a white beard and a rather stern countenance. Appointed nearly ten years before, he had changed much of the smash-and-grab archaeology that Egypt was known for under men like Maspero, preferring historical preservation. Needless to say, he disapproved of men like my employer.

"Bonjour, Monsieur Director," I began, cutting off the windy breath Royale started out with. "Would you like some tea?"

"I would, yes," he replied, unbending so far as to let his mouth curl up at the corners.

"So what's this all about, Lacau?" Royale asked. "I would have thought you'd still be fighting with Carter."

Howard Carter, the discoverer of King Tutankhamen, had caused a great deal of distress to the bureau, especially with his whole refusal to let anyone but the *Times* of London carry stories about his tomb. Personally, I thought he was mad, as it put his entire concession into jeopardy.

"Ah, yes. Well, that is part of why I am here. The Egyptian press wants to have some of its own stories, and while we cannot easily give them Carter, we can try to put a good face on what else is happening." Lacau took the barest sip of his tea, grimaced at the taste, and set it aside.

I could not blame him. The stuff tasted like boiled oil.

"We have work to do," Royale argued. "We haven't got time for all this flapdoodle and claptrap."

Lacau simply stared until Royale coughed and backed down a bit. Then he replied quite evenly, "This will take no more than a half hour. Show me about the dig, if you please."

They were gone in the blink of an eye, and I sighed, for Marion had stayed behind.

"So, how is Aunt Hettie?" I asked, speaking of my mother's aunt, Marion's mother.

"Somewhat frail, I fear. But not so much that I am needed at home." He was eyeing me in a very avuncular way, ready to pounce with concern and good advice, no doubt.

"I am sorry to hear that." By Gad, that tea was terrible. It had me sweating, pulling at my collar to loosen it. "And my brother? How is Sebastian?"

"Quite well. Enjoying the bucolic life. His wife is pregnant."

"What, again? Good heavens. He should let up on her." My brother and I rarely spoke, but I knew he had three children already.

"Undoubtedly." Marion chattered on about family for some time. Finally he drew himself up and just asked what was on his mind. "Christian, are you quite sure you know what you're getting into?"

"What, with Royale? He's a brash American is all," I said, trying to sound convincing. "Nothing bad will come of it."

"There are rumors, lad. Dark ones."

"Bah." I tried my best to remain stoic in the face of his shrewd regard. "People talk, and thanks to Carter, there are many, many rumors about this season."

"Yes, well, this seems to have merit. There is talk that he and Zavigny are racing to find some heretofore unknown artifact."

"If they are, I know nothing about it," I replied, keeping myself from looking away by dint of sheer will. I would not have him knowing I lied.

"Well, keep your eyes and ears open. This sort of land

war can get vicious." He leaned forward, the very picture of earnestness. "I am very proud of you, Christian. Do not allow yourself to be dragged down now."

"I assure you, all is well."

Thank God the Director General returned then with Royale. I drained the last of my tea and stood, swaying a bit.

"Is there anything you require, sir?" I asked, my mouth feeling fuzzy, my tongue thick.

"No, no," Royale grumbled. "They seem to have it well in hand. Good Lord, boy, you look like you're about to fall down."

"I believe I am," I agreed as the world spun, and then I fell into darkness, hearing Marion shout my name just before I blacked out.

14

———

"Who in hell made that tea, that's what I wanna know!"

I woke to a terrible pounding in my head, the sun trying to break through my eyelids so it might dry my eyeballs like dates.

The voice sounded like Eric's, but I had trouble believing it. What I could remember last was being with the Director General and Marion, so how had I gotten to Zavigny's camp?

"I don't know! No one admitted to it, and the cook was not in the tent then. I saw him myself, out with the men." The heavy accent could only mean Silad, my headman. So where was I?

"Excuse me," I tried to say, my throat feeling as though I had swallowed a broken bottle. "Where am I?"

"Just relax, Chrissy. You're safe." Someone, presumably Lawless, plopped a slimy, wet cloth on my forehead. My hand rose automatically to claw it away, and I could not help but open my eyes then to stare at my shaking hand. I was weak as a kitten.

"Where. Am. I?"

"You are still in camp, sayyid," Silad replied. "Lawless came to check on you when the Director General reached his camp. Would you like water? I drew it myself."

"Nice to know some things remain on schedule," I quipped, nodding and reaching for the dipper Silad held out. "How long...?"

"You've been out a whole day," Lawless said. "I been worried about you."

"I see why. May I have more water, please?"

Silad gave me the water, and I felt marginally better, the pain in my throat easing. "What happened?"

"We think it was the tea," Silad replied, cutting his eyes to look at Lawless.

"The tea." The tea. Had it been poisoned?

"The director?"

"He's fine. He went on to old Zaffiggy's camp with no more than a bit of a bellyache. We didn't say nothin', but of course, when you went down, a hundred press folks were standing around. We got us another mummy's curse."

"How ridiculous when we haven't a mummy," I murmured. "Excuse me."

With that I bent over the side of the bunk and was violently ill, the water not sitting on my stomach at all.

When I woke the second time, the light was not nearly so bright, coming from the soft glow of a lamp rather than the sun. My eyes did not protest at all when I opened them, and while my throat was still raw, I was much improved.

There was someone sitting next to my bed, very close by. In fact, that someone had their head down on my bed, and they were snoring.

I assumed that ruled out Mr. Royale.

"There you are," Eric said, and I blinked to bring him into focus.

"Aren't you supposed to be organizing Professor Zavigny's security or some such?" I asked.

"Zaffiggy wants me here with you. He figures he needs you to help him out."

That fact had not escaped me even when I was busy enough not to think on it. Now I had nothing but time, and I found it quite odd.

"He has people on his staff far better trained than I. Why me?"

"I dunno." Stretching, Eric popped his back and neck before shrugging. "Maybe he wants to give you a chance."

He looked so tired, the circles under his eyes almost as dark as the gray irises in them. Looking at him, I was struck by how dear his face had become, despite his most maddening tendencies. I reached out to him, and he took my hand, stroking the back idly.

"You should sleep."

"Ah, hell, Chrissy. I been watching over you. If someone was trying to poison you, they might try again."

"Oh, I should think they were after the Director General. Luckily for him, he is unused to the sludge we call tea out here."

"Uh-huh." He did not sound at all convinced, but I felt positive I was correct. Even earlier incidents could not convince me that the tea was aimed at me. There had been too good a chance I would not even drink it.

"How badly have the press taken hold of this?"

"They're running with it like a mustang with the bit in his teeth," Eric replied. "I tell you what, Chrissy. I see one more of them crawling out here like flies and I'll shoot 'em."

"You will so no such thing. Can you imagine the trouble

we'd have then?" I thought on that for a bit before I remembered to ask about the map and statuette. "My bag. Is it...?"

"Safe. That Silad is a good man. First thing he did was secure your tent, just in case."

"I want to see them."

He gave me a look but said nothing, simply rising and going to get my bag. I confess, I admired the way his trousers stretched over his backside, even though I had no strength to do anything about it.

"There, you see? All there." He produced the map case and the strange black figure, and I nodded with relief.

"Excellent. Thank you."

Lawless gave me a pleased smile, the lines on his face easing. "You're welcome. Am I gonna hurt you if I kiss you?"

"No. In fact, I think I might demand that you do."

His kiss was slow, gentle, and easy, just a long touch of his lips to mine. Nothing demanding came out of it, and it did not further the ache in my head, thank God.

When it was done, I had him put the relics away and held out my hand. "Come sleep with me. You can wake before dawn easily enough."

"I always do."

"Yes, then come on." I wanted him against me, wanted his solid presence, and I felt he needed to rest as badly as I did. He would wake should something happen.

How odd it was that, no matter what our start, he was the one person in the world I had begun to trust above all others.

15

When I awoke the next morning, feeling like all I did anymore was sleep, Lawless was gone. In his place I found Marion Keyes, staring at me as if willing me to come to.

"Good morning, lad! Good to see you awake," he boomed, causing me to wince.

"Good morning, Marion. Might I use the necessary before you start in on me?"

I could not recall the last time I had gone, and I chose to see the fact that I needed to rather strongly as a good sign. A true recovery.

His cheeks went bright red, and he nodded, rising. "Of course, of course. I'll just step outside, shall I?"

"If you please."

Once he was out, I checked to make sure my bag was not where he could have easily rummaged the contents. Lawless, bless his heart, had pushed it all the way back under my cot, where it was unlikely anyone could get to it without waking me.

I used the pot, then pushed it outside and wobbled back to my bed, where I sat rather harder than I intended.

"Still feeling the effects, eh?" Marion said when he came back in.

"Apparently, yes. I feel miles better than I did, though."

"Good, good. You caused quite a stir, lad." He handed me a stack of papers, all of them bearing fantastic titles like "The Mummy Strikes Again" and "Curse Breaks Out on Expedition."

"Oh good God," I said, leafing through them. "Well, I suppose it's a mercy that the Director General was unharmed."

"Yes, yes, indeed. Christian, the director has asked me to implore you. What is going on out here?"

"Whatever do you mean?" My voice stayed light, even. I was most proud.

"You have Americans gallivanting about. Both Royale and Zavigny have been exceedingly closemouthed. And now you have been poisoned. There is something deeply wrong here, especially when you're in what should be the least active part of the valley."

"Pshaw." Trying to wave him off produced nothing but a floppy arm on my part. Using the pot had left me drained. "Marion, that's a load of codswallop. It's simply been a run of bad luck. And I say if anyone was poisoned, it was meant for the director. Probably a Carter supporter. I just happen to be a tea addict."

"I see. Well, it's clear you will not tell me." Marion stood, clapping a pith helmet on his head. "Let me at least give you a piece of advice, then, lad."

"What's that?" I asked cautiously.

"Your American friend, Lawless. He is far too demonstrative. Have him keep at least at arm's length, hmm?"

With that he was gone, leaving me staring for long moments at the flap of my tent. When no one else came, I slept.

16

————

The king sat on his throne, still as a statue, his tall crown glinting in the firelight. He watched impassively as the dark man with eyes like holes in the sky waved his arms and chanted, a scroll open before him on a carved black table.

The room filled with smoke, heavy with herbs, and as the dark man called upon the forces of the gods, dark forms began to take shape in the corners of the room.

Each one resolved itself into the form of a great, shaggy hound with glowing red eyes. Each came to the dark man and rested their heads against him, waiting. Staring.

The man turned to the king, demanding the names of all those who had defied the king's need for more sacrifices.

When the king spoke, his lips barely moved, and his voice was reedy as an old man's.

Then the dark man turned and sent each hound on its way with a man to hunt. With a name to strike out of the book of souls forever.

I was not then a man given to fanciful dreams. So when I woke to yet another one, the fourth in a week, I made it a point to take time to ponder what they might mean. I sat at the dining tent, the irony of that not lost on me. I made my own tea.

Though still not back to fighting trim, I felt more than recovered enough to be back to work. I had examined the site the day before, checking after Silad, which I needn't have, really. The only thing that concerned me was the men. They worked in a sullen silence, no singing to be heard. That usually meant trouble.

I had asked Silad about it, and his answer was that no one liked the attention from the press. After a week or so, however, that died down, and things began to get back to normal.

So why were the men so silent?

Between the sleepless nights and the nerve-racking days, I admit, I tired easily. So when I sat to try to make heads or tails of my dreams, I made no progress.

Instead I thought of Lawless. I missed him, both his face and his touch. He was a canny man, and I had no doubt he had overheard or heard elsewhere what Marion had said. That rumors were circulating. No doubt he wanted to give them time to cool off, but I wanted to see him. Badly.

Finally I simply set myself to writing down the recurring facts of the dreams to share with him later. The king looked like the classic statues of Osiris, the once King of All Egypt and ruler of the underworld. In fact, his face looked exactly like that on the little golden statue Zavigny possessed. The dark man was no doubt the little black statue, despite the differences in shape.

So what did all the hokum about sacrificing and weird animals have to do with it?

Royale, for his part, had ignored me of late. I wondered if he thought I would ask for more money as hazard pay.

Now, though, I saw him approaching and casually closed my notebook.

He cleared his throat loudly. "So. How are you, boy?"

"Much improved, sir," I replied. "What news?"

"Bah." He spat in the dirt at his feet. "The Director General wants to do a real inspection now. Something about one of the reporters talking to the men about a find here. Damnation! That's the last thing we need, boy!"

"Have you found something else?"

"No," he said immediately, but his eyes slid away from mine, his cheeks going deep pink.

"Ah. So now you would hide it even from me?"

"What you don't know they can't ask of you," he said, his shoulders rolling.

"Or it could get me killed. Is that an acceptable risk?"

He sighed. "All right, all right. But not here and not now. I'll fill you in tonight. Meet me at the Frenchie's tent."

It was almost comical, the way he tried to lower his booming voice. For my part I only nodded, knowing this was a great concession for him.

"Very well. I shall do that."

"Eight o'clock," he said. "Don't be late, boy."

Really, I thought as he left. It had been the strangest couple of days.

17

I met Lawless on the way to Zavigny's camp. He was armed to the teeth, and I could only stare.

"Are we going to a shoot-out?" I asked.

"No. But I ain't taking no chances with you, Chrissy. Too many weird things have been happening."

"I was just thinking that this morning," I murmured.

He nodded, eyes searching the barren expanse of terrain, shadowed by the darkness, lit only by the rising moon.

"It's nearly eight," I said when he did not immediately move on. "Royale told me not to be late."

"Uh-huh." With one more look about, Lawless grabbed me suddenly and yanked me to him, kissing me until stars swam in my field of vision. He let me go just as suddenly.

I staggered, bouncing off a rock and sitting down rather suddenly. "Ow."

"Sorry," he said, holding a hand down to help me up. "Missed you."

The gruff tone of his voice told me it was true, and I

laughed a little, the sound bouncing a bit. "I missed you too. Shall we go to our gathering of the minds?"

"Yeah, we ought."

We said very little while we walked, and soon enough we were at Zavigny's tent. More armed men, Europeans and Americans, stood about, dotting the landscape like bizarre armored bugs.

Interesting.

I took the offensive when I reached Zavigny and Royale, who sat just far enough apart that one could read the antagonism in their body language.

"Very well," I said. "I insist that you tell me what is going on."

Zavigny jumped and Royale scowled, and I would not have changed my tack, though I knew I had put their backs up.

"That damned director's visit has made it impossible to work," Royale said.

"At least with any degree of secrecy," Zavigny agreed, nodding like one of those awful cast-iron toys.

"And you both feel we have something to hide." Ah, honest and aboveboard, that was the theme of Lacau, the Director General. Too bad my employers did not subscribe to it. My own moral fiber was not stern, per se, but I felt superior to them, then.

"Well, look at this...."

It was Zavigny who lifted the cover off the relic, his Gallic temperament requiring that he do it with a flourish, like a matador with a bull.

As if I were a character in a silent movie, I stumbled back, hand going to my mouth. I could not have been more dramatic if I was June Marlowe. Still, to see a piece of throne carved out of stone, little bits of plaster and gold still adhering to it, was a shock. It was exactly as I had seen it in my dream.

"Where did you find this?" I whispered. "Surely not on our dig."

Lawless stared at me, and I could almost feel his concern and curiosity like a physical touch. He stayed silent, though, leaving the others to speak.

"Not on our digs, no," Zavigny said. "But if it makes you feel better, not on anyone else's permit either. This was found between here and the mouth of the West Valley."

The West Valley. Where the map led to some hereto unknown tomb. My God. I opened my mouth to speak, but Lawless nudged my arm, shooting me a look. Yes. Perhaps best not to mention the map.

"You think this ties in with the other artifacts?"

"How can it not?" Zavigny asked, waving a hand at the piece of throne. "It is the same stone as the statuette. The glyphs... look how they have been chiseled off. I think this is all part and parcel of a single burial, only they wanted to separate the pieces. Either through thievery or very deliberately."

Royale's eyes gleamed. "One way or the other, that means there's some hefty treasure just waiting to be found, and we're the only ones with concessions in this area."

"A concession is not a blanket. No wonder the Director General was here."

Nothing this large could be discovered without some scuttlebutt going about. It had obviously reached the highest levels, and this was serious enough to bring out the rule makers en masse.

"*Oui*," Zavigny agreed. "If there is more to be found, we must do it quickly. Do you see why we are desperate?"

"What I don't see," Eric broke in, drawling offensively, "is how y'all started working together. I thought it was every man for himself. And God knows y'all seemed like big dogs to begin with, pissing on your own plot of ground. Why the sudden change of heart?"

As if they had forgotten he was there, both Royale and Zavigny turned to stare at Eric. He did not wither at all under their looks, simply leaning back on a map table, crossing his booted feet at the ankle.

"We share a common goal, if not common reasoning or methodology," Zavigny finally said. "We both have reasons we'd rather not have the bureau among us."

"Uh-huh. And I'm thinking it's time you explained those reasons to Chrissy here."

"Bullshit!" Royale boomed. "I'm not explaining shit for my reasons. It's enough for him to know what's going on. We need you, lad. Actively searching for this stuff. Stop mucking about on the dig and start mapping the path between here and the West Valley."

"Ah." Yes, it made sense now. Out of everyone on their staff, I was the only one who could do the work and not make waves. Silad was a fine headman, but his loyalty lay with the people and preservation of Egypt, so they could not ask him. And Lawless was not a digger.

"Well, my boy?" Zavigny asked. "Are you up for the adventure?"

Lawless stared at me keenly, his gray eyes like smoke, obscuring whatever he thought of the idea.

If I could have said no, I would have, but I knew as well as they that I was already too deep in this mess and could not walk away. So I only nodded.

"Yes," I said. "Count me in."

18

———

"I got a bad feeling about this, Chrissy," Eric said, taking my elbow when I would have started back to my own camp and steering me toward his tent.

We had gotten through the better part of a tactical meeting, the professor showing me charts and grids, explaining where each artifact, including the little golden statue of Osiris, had been found.

How Royale had blustered then about Zavigny "holding out on him."

"So you've said," I finally agreed. "I fear I am not completely confident either, but what can I do?" I spread my hands, shrugging. "I need the job, and it could advance me in the field, certainly."

"Or get you dead."

Once inside the tent, he lit a lamp and then unbuckled his gun belt and removed the many other weapons on his person. Then I was in his arms, my shocked gasp the only sound before our lips met. His speed and need astonished me, the press of his lips bruising in its force.

My hands cupped the back of his neck and clung, my hips beginning to rock with no thought or permission from me, moving my prick back and forth across his thigh. The cloth between us felt hot, itchy, and stifling, and I began to tear at his clothes.

His skin became a feast I could dine on all night. When his shirt hit the floor of the tent, I let out a little sound of satisfaction, and he laughed at me.

Eric stopped laughing when I bent to bite at one tiny nipple, however. Then he groaned for me. The sound had me searching for more hot spots, my lips traveling over his chest, my fingers finding his flat belly and stroking down to the waist of his trousers.

He had the most beautiful skin. Tanned and smooth, with just enough hair to lend texture, it called to my hands. I touched him hungrily, needing more, and it shocked my whole body when he tore me away.

"Clothes, Chrissy. Lose them."

His grin gleamed feral in the low light, making him look predatory, fully a male animal.

Nodding, I stripped off while he went to work on his trousers and boots, and we smacked back together in the center of the tent, skin on skin.

We both moaned then, rubbing furiously, and my cock caught on his, the tip catching on the underside of Eric's shaft. I grunted, going up on tiptoes, and Eric caught us both in one hand, stroking.

At once too much and not enough, the touch galvanized me. I arched against him, rocking into the touch, licking the sweat from his neck. His taste spurred me on, and all I could do was strive for more, for right now, for my need to be quenched.

I spent myself so quickly that I shook when I was done,

the shivers running up and down my spine as I slumped against him.

"God, Chrissy. Please. I need." He still moved against me, his arm swinging madly, and I added my trembling touch to his, squeezing hard and pulling from root to tip.

Crying out, Lawless came for me, against me, his seed coating my skin. The scent of him slammed into me, making me whimper, and I kissed him, then, with all the pent-up passion I had held since our last meeting, far too long before.

We sank to the floor of the tent, holding one another closely, both of us silent.

Then he started to chuckle.

"What?" I asked, striving for haughty and achieving no more than slightly querulous.

"Well, that didn't go as planned, lover," he replied. "I was gonna go slow and easy."

"Ah. Well, we still have time for that, I assure you."

"Do we? Well, good deal." His laughter was infectious, and soon I found myself joining him, the tension of the day draining away.

"Come on, lover. We got us a cot. We might as well use it."

I felt like a rag doll while he moved us to the bed, floppy and useless as any poppet. Eric seemed not to mind, so I merely curled against him, kissing his bristly chin.

"Do you think—?" I began, but he stopped me with a finger to my lips.

"No work. Not now. Let it go for tonight."

Yes, I supposed I could do that. I settled more firmly against him, fingers tracing a scar on his chest.

"Tell me where you got this, then."

"A knife fight in Abilene."

"A knife fight! How droll." I tried to keep my tone light, but my God, I thought. He could have been killed.

"Hey, I didn't start it. I didn't have a knife to fight back with until someone in the crowd gave me one. I was just minding my own business, playing cards...."

"Are you saying trouble follows you?"

"I got you, don't I?"

"Oh!" Pinching the skin on his upper arm, I laughed at him. "You would be here regardless."

"Yeah, so it's a good thing I got you to liven it up."

"Yes." I had no wish to think what would happen when we parted at the end of the season, so I moved on.

"And this?" I asked, poking a round, raised scar on his hip.

"Boarding house fire. Some damned fool thought some other damned fool had stolen his dancing girl. He set the place ablaze, and I ended up carrying out the lady owner. All three hundred pounds of her."

"You're a good man, Eric Lawless."

"Shit, lover. I'm just a hired gun."

Lawless pulled me up against him, hitching me up on his chest so he could kiss me, cutting off further questioning, no doubt.

How could I blame him when I remained just as reticent about my own past?

We kissed long and thoroughly, both of us gasping for breath when we parted, only to dive right back in. Even though we had barely finished, the heat rose between us again, both of us beginning to move, this time more able to touch, to taste.

Eric held me with one hand, his other tracing down my spine to cup my bottom. "Wanna ride me, lover?"

His crudeness had my prick leaping. I had once

despaired for him with his rude language. Now it enflamed me.

"Yes. Please. Have you anything?"

We seemed to have this discussion every time, and while I was prepared now with oil, it seemed this time he was not, for he shook his head. "I spilled the oil that went with my strop."

"Then I should beat you with said strop, hmm?"

"You try it and I'll tan your ass," he said, whapping me.

"Oh, very well." I licked my fingers and reached behind myself, running my fingers down between my cheeks. Preparation took far longer than I would have liked, for it had been at least two weeks. Finally my muscles relaxed, though, and I was able to work two fingers in.

I looked up to find him watching me, his whole form still beneath me. "What?" I asked, striving for a casual mien.

"That's the most amazing thing I've ever seen, darlin'," he answered. "Makes me hard as a rock."

"Ah, the feeling is mutual, then." I worked myself harder, striving to be as open and easy for him as I could. Once I thought I was relaxed enough, I spat into my palm and reached for his cock.

Smooth, silky, the skin there was so hot it was like the sun had risen in the tent. I stroked him, up and down until he finally grabbed my hand.

"You're gonna use up the wet," he said. "Come on, Chrissy."

Giving his nipple an evil pinch, I rose up over him, the cot swaying precariously beneath us.

"Are you ready?"

"Hell, yes." Grabbing my hips, he tried to force me down. "Hell, yes. Come on, lover. Now."

I straddled him, my thighs on either side of his hips, and

moved up until the head of his cock pushed under my balls. Then I reached back and settled the thick head of his prick against my hole, utterly enflamed by the feeling of him inside me.

My prick ached, bobbing up and down crazily when I sank down on him. I moaned when he filled me, hot as a poker and just as hard as iron, his hips poking into my legs.

"Eric," I said, and to my own ears my voice sounded drugged. Poisoned tea be damned, this was what was going to kill me.

"Yeah, lover. Yeah. Come on."

His hands encouraged the movements of my hips even while mine landed on his chest for leverage. My short nails dug in, the hair on his chest curling about them, and I laughed, pushing my head back and sitting down as hard as I could with my bottom.

He made a noise that could have been a curse or a prayer, grabbing my cock and pulling at it. We became a full circle of pleasure, one that couldn't be denied.

I rode him, just as he'd said. I moved on him like I couldn't not. Like it was a compulsion. My body jerked gracelessly above him. When his thumb dragged against my pulled-back foreskin, I released for him, spending myself completely, everything in me pouring out.

Lawless gave no more than a silent, shocked gasp, his eyes wide when he bucked under me. He filled me to bursting, his prick throbbing deep within me, and I could not have asked for more. My name fell from his lips when he finished, slumping back against the cot as if he could no longer hold his head up.

I fell upon him, panting, sweat running on my skin.

"Oh, lover...."

Dragging my head up, I smiled at him. "Yes."

He patted my back clumsily. "Sleep. I'll wake you when it's time to get back to camp."

Trusting in him, I let myself go, slipping away into sleep. I had no doubt he would do whatever he said. Lawless was a man of his word.

19

———

Something woke me in the shadows before dawn, and at first I thought it was only Lawless shaking me awake. His hand upon my shoulder simply lay there gently, and I smiled, stretching.

Which was when I realized that Eric still slept beneath me, his chest rising and falling evenly.

Looking over my shoulder, I saw a monstrous shadow, three times the size of anything that should have fit in a tiny tent. Gasping, I flung myself away, rolling off the cot and landing on the ground, banging my elbow on the leg of the bed hard enough to see stars for a moment.

That had Eric sitting straight up on the cot, a pistol appearing from thin air, it seemed.

"Chrissy?"

"Look."

I pointed with a trembling finger, and he bit out a curse, cocking the pistol. "What the fuck is that?"

Even as part of my brain chastised him for the foul word, the rest of me agreed. Indeed. The shadows shifted constantly, each form more foul than the next. I could not tear my eyes away, and yet it hurt to watch.

As if pulled one by one from the ethereal mist like ribbons of smoke, words began to form. "Find the king," the thing said. "Free the king."

"Oh, I don't think so." Lawless would have pulled the trigger then had I not caught his arm.

"No! Do you want the whole camp upon us?"

He never looked away from the apparition, but he said through gritted teeth, "If it gets rid of this, then yeah."

"No. It won't." Somehow I knew it. I'm not sure how I knew, but in light of recent events, I was willing to trust my instincts.

"Then what do we do?"

"We listen."

The shifting shape seemed to laugh at us, a gaping maw opening where a head might belong, shining, sharp teeth appearing. The alien horror of it dragged goose bumps up my skin. My fingers dug harder into Eric's arm.

"Release the king," the thing intoned once more, and the mass of it disintegrated, falling like shattered glass to the floor of the tent and becoming a hundred scuttling centipedes, the thousands of tiny legs moving and wiggling like a pile of maggots before they too disappeared.

"Goddamn," Eric said, staring at the floor as if waiting for a chance to shoot something.

"Indeed. Well, that was certainly not the best way to start the day."

He turned his incredulous stare on me. "Not the.... You sure are calm about this, lover. Did you *see* that thing?"

"Well, of course I did," I snarled, feeling somewhat cross. "But then, I've been seeing things just like it in my dreams for more than a fortnight."

"More than... you've been holding out on me, Chrissy. Tell."

Lawless pulled me into his arms, letting me lean against his solid chest, his heartbeat thumping far too quickly against me.

So I told him.

"The king seems to figure heavily in them," I finished some minutes later. "I'm not so certain that unearthing him is a good idea."

"Well, someone sure wants him found."

"Yes."

We sat in silence for a long while, both of us lost in our thoughts. Then Eric placed a kiss on my shoulder. "Whattaya say we find this old king and burn the mummy or something?"

It went against every bit of my training to agree, but agree I did. "I think that's a fine idea. We'll start looking in earnest tomorrow."

20

I made my way back to Royale's camp early in the morning. Eric insisted upon accompanying me, but he did turn back once my tent was in sight. It was a good thing, for I felt I needed some quiet time to ponder the events of the previous evening.

How much did Royale and Zavigny know about what they were looking for? This question seemed paramount. On the surface it seemed they were completely unaware. While I could believe this of Royale, I felt Zavigny had to be suspect, for he was no fool.

Sitting on my cot in the barest light of the early morning, I pulled out my sketchbook and began to jot down a timeline of what had occurred since I had arrived in Egypt. It was a grim picture, a pattern I could not believe I had been so blind to. I had been herded into this entire venture, and very deliberately.

As it stood, I had three choices. I could pack my things and leave Luxor. I could go about the dig as it was and find the bloody king, just as my employers wanted to. Or Lawless and I could find the king and destroy him forever.

Predictably I decided on the latter.

Pulling the map case out of my bag, along with the little statue of the black man, I studied both in detail. That the black man was the figure of my dreams I had no doubt, but I could not find a single reference to him in any of my tomes of ancient lore. Osiris's brother Set was often referred to as a black man with red hair, but this creature had tentacles in place of a head, and that was unheard of.

Alternatively the map made more sense. We had done enough hiking in that area now that I began to see landmarks that had hitherto gone unnoticed. In fact, I then realized that the map must indeed be a copy of an antique, only it was modernized to reflect the changed landscape. My mind had tried to see it as it once must have been, which had been my error. Now I thought I might well be able to walk right to the tomb's entrance.

God, what a fool I had been all along.

I sat there, shivering, trying to make sense of it all, until it was time for me to go and join Silad for the day's planning.

I bathed quickly and put on a fresh suit of clothes before going to meet Silad. To my surprise, I found him alone at the kitchen tent, his face as long as an afternoon shadow.

"What's wrong, Silad?"

"The men have gone," he said, holding out his arms, hands palms up.

"What? All of them? Where?"

"Only your white men remain," he said. "They snuck out in the night."

"My God."

"What shall we do, sayyid? We cannot dig with no diggers."

Deep lines bracketed Silad's mouth, worn there by more

than one morning's worry, and I chastised myself for not noticing sooner.

"Tell me what has happened, Silad. I have been neglecting my duties here."

He rolled his shoulders and his eyes in the eloquent way of the Arab. "The men have heard rumors."

"Not that ridiculous curse nonsense from my, er, accident, I trust."

"No. That they understand. That was someone trying to kill you."

I stared at him. "The poison was meant for the Director of Antiquities."

"As you say, sayyid."

Which meant exactly the opposite. He believed that tea was meant for me alone, something I still refused to contemplate.

"What, then?"

"They have heard that we are looking for the tomb of Osiris himself. They believe when he is unearthed, the war with his brother will begin once more and bring the fall of Egypt."

"Osiris is a myth."

"You and Allah know this is true," Silad agreed. "But many of the diggers still fear the old ways. What is it Sallah Abu Deen tells me? Myths have power if people believe."

Yes, I could see Silad's mentor saying such things. And did it not have power over me? I believed in my premonitions.

"We shall simply have to hire more diggers, then. Mr. Royale will not abide a slowdown."

"But where?" Silad spread his hands again, the gesture radiating futility. "The effendi does not understand. No one from the villages will come now."

"Then we will simply have to put some of the pampered white guards to work, hmm?" I smiled at him, receiving a tentative smile in return. "Did they take all of the food as well?"

"No, sayyid. They are not thieves."

"Of course not. They did not wait to be paid, though, so I thought they might take it as their due."

We stared at one another a moment before I rose, wiping my clammy hands on my trousers. "Well. We should get the men we have left to work. I suggest we concentrate on the grid closest to the West Valley."

He cut his eyes at me but only nodded. "Yes, sayyid."

The guards grumbled at having to do manual labor, but I quelled them with a look, directing the few men to get started and leaving them in Silad's capable hands.

I made my way to Royale's tent, steeling myself to explain that he had lost all the men, including his valet.

To my surprise, I found him sitting on the stool outside his tent, his head in his hands. When he peered up at me, his red-rimmed eyes shocked me.

"Are you well, sir?"

"Do I look well? What do you want, Christian?"

"The men have left, sir."

"Well, I'm not stupid, am I, boy? I knew that."

"Oh." I paused, searching for my next gambit. "Silad is fairly certain that we will not be able to get new ones."

"Well, that's that, eh, lad? Maybe we can borrow some from old Frenchie."

"I suppose that is possible, if they have not staged a walkout of their own." The two camps were too directly linked for me to believe that what one group did, the other would not.

"I suppose they might have."

Really, he seemed so tired and dejected, so unlike his usual boisterous self, that I was moved to concern.

"What can I do for you, sir?"

His eyes met mine with the force of a physical blow. "You just find that goddamned tomb."

"Yes, sir," I said, feeling the weight of his stare like a stone on my chest. "I have every intention of it."

21

———————

I sent Silad with the message for Eric. I did not trust anyone else to make sure it arrived, and he would be able to speak to Zavigny's headman about borrowing workers.

When he returned, his expression was even more grim than it had been early in the morning.

"I am sorry, sayyid. The professor effendi is no better than we are. His men have gone."

"I was afraid of that."

"Your friend says he will come."

"Thank you, Silad."

He left me to whip our remaining workers into shape, and I made the men a meal, tasting the food carefully for any signs of poison.

The day dragged interminably, and we gave the men the rest of the day off at the midday meal, for they all complained of blisters and heat exhaustion. After that, I had little to do but pace and fret until Eric arrived.

He came near twilight, fully armed, his hat pulled down

over his eyes. "You ready, Chrissy?" he asked, scratching his bristly chin.

"As ready as can be, I suspect. Shall we?"

Our mission set, we made for the West Valley, the sound of our boots ringing on stone the only thing we heard. Even the birds seemed to have stilled. The eerie silence was not lost on Lawless, who kept his guard up quite well, examining every shadow as though a threat lay in its center.

The trip took a good bit out of me, for though I felt mostly recovered, I was not entirely up to snuff. Even Lawless had taken on a limp by the time we reached the head trail shown on the map, his ankle apparently bothering him.

"This is the beginning of the map," I said, breaking the oppressive silence. "We go this way."

"Are you sure?"

The map had been burned into my mind indelibly once I sorted it out, so I nodded. "I'm sure."

He followed me closely, fairly breathing down my neck. I could not blame him. The trail narrowed so drastically in places that either of us could have fallen, and the farther we trekked, the less light we had, the rising moon the only illumination.

It looked as though no tomb could possibly fit among the sheer walls of the canyon, but I knew it was so. When I began to see familiar landmarks, I slowed, trailing my fingers along the rock wall.

"What are we looking for, Chrissy?"

"Unnatural fissures," I said, ignoring the hated nickname. "Anything man-made. Remember, many of their accomplishments are as impressive architecturally as anything we have today. We're not looking for a crude hole. It will be subtle."

"Right. Because subtlety is my strong suit."

I glanced over my shoulder just in time to see the white of his smile, and I could not help but laugh. "Oh, yes. You are the soul of couth."

"What the hell is that?"

Laughing harder, I turned to him, minding where I put my feet. "Kiss me?"

"Oh, lover, you don't have to beg for kisses." His hands fell on my shoulders, his lips meeting mine hard and fast.

Moaning, I opened to him, loving the taste of him on my tongue, the feel of his mouth moving on mine.

I let the kisses go on far longer than I should have, no doubt, but I needed them badly. They were at once reassuring and engulfing, sending all my worries spinning off into space, and I reveled in it. In him.

When he let me go, we both panted for breath, only standing there and leaning on one another. Finally, though, he set me from him.

"Let's find that damned tomb," he said. "I want this over with so we can just get the hell out of Dodge."

"And where would we get away to, love?"

"We could take one of them river cruises. You can spout history to the touring folks, and I can work."

The fact that Eric wished to take me with him when he left created a tumult in me. And it was a good idea, as well, working the cruises that ran down, then up, the Nile. It would certainly get us away from the drama of the Carter and Carnarvon crew. I kissed him again then, slow and sure, letting him feel my gratitude.

"That is a fine idea, Eric. Thank you."

"Well, let's get at it, then."

The map became no help once we found the general area where the mouth of the tomb supposedly sat. There was no landmark or X to mark the spot, and we were essentially working blind, as dark as it was. We had to do a great deal by feel.

"Be careful, Chrissy. There could be more snakes."

"Or other traps," I agreed.

We worked for nearly an hour, canvassing the entire face of the wall that was within our reach, when finally Lawless began to climb, his feet and hands finding only the most precarious holds. When I would have protested, he shushed me.

"I swear to God, Chrissy, you make me fall and kill myself, I'll haunt you into eternity, and you won't need no spooky king."

I clapped my hand over my mouth to stifle my shout of laughter. Gracious, that man had a turn of phrase. To think I had once found him willfully ignorant.

A long silence followed, punctuated only by the sounds of the night and the occasional fall of dirt and stone under Lawless's boots. I chewed my thumbnail, a habit I had given up in my school days when the headmaster had coated my nails with ipecac. Really, he was taking the longest—

"Chrissy! I think I got something."

Peering up to where he hung on the wall like a human fly, I watched his hand disappear into a large fissure.

"Be careful. I could just be a fault in the stone."

"No. There's all sorts of marks and shit, stonework marks. And back beyond there's something smooth and hard, something not rock."

"Can you mark the opening so it can be seen from below? We'll have to come back with ropes and tools."

"Or some dynamite," he grumbled. "Yeah. Yeah, I can mark it."

There came a great flurry of grunting and scrabbling,

and he nearly hit me with a rock the size of my head, but Lawless managed to mark the entry with his red handkerchief weighted down with a large stone.

Surefooted as a goat, Lawless was beside me again in moments, the descent far shorter than the ascent.

"That ought to hold it until tomorrow," he said.

"Good. We should go and get some rest."

Faced now with the prospect of actually knowing the tomb's location, I began to fear what we might find. My resolve did not waver, but I admit my courage did.

Lawless looked at me, carefully scrutinizing me despite the darkness. "No losing your nerve now, Chrissy. It's too late for that."

"I know!" I snapped. "I simply dislike being pushed into anything. Royale and Zavigny have been using me all along, and now some supernatural being has a hand in, and it makes me quite angry."

Kissing my nose, he laughed. "And that makes you cute as hell."

"Do not patronize me." But I could not help but smile. "We're going to need help."

"Well, I don't think we can trust old Zaffiggy or Royale."

"No, but we can trust Silad. He's a good man, and he knows something is afoot. He will help us."

I hated to involve Silad if there was danger afoot like I supposed, but he was not a stupid man, and he deserved first crack at anything in that tomb save the mummy, if there was one.

"Well then, you talk with him in the morning while I supply us."

"Yes. Yes, that will do nicely."

We left then, making the long trek back to camp, and

though I was physically exhausted, my mind felt too alive to sleep. I grabbed Lawless's hand when he would have left me.

"Stay?" I asked, feeling selfish and small.

"You know I will."

With hardly another word, we made our way back to my tent, Eric pulling his gun and checking every corner before drawing me in.

His kisses held the same fine sense of desperation I felt, his mouth sealing over mine so he might steal my breath and make my head spin.

I clutched him to me, my hands pulling at his shirt, the straps of his various holsters. His skin appeared inch by inch, and when I pulled away from his kiss, I stopped his protest with touches and kisses to all of those other spots, tasting dust and sweat on his skin.

Scrapes dotted his hands and arms and even his chest, and I kissed each one, giving them a hero's due.

Eric moaned and twisted under my touch, his hands pushing at me, tearing at my clothes. I did not want to let go long enough to disrobe, but he finally broke free. The sound of my shirt ripping echoed through the tent.

"Sorry," he murmured, but he didn't seem sorry at all, his fingers exploring my chest, plucking at my nipples.

Moving against him was pure bliss, and by the time we were both nude, we were ravenous. I bit at his collarbone and he grabbed my bottom and we slapped together over and over until he finally went to his knees before me.

Surprised, I stared down at him while he grinned up at me, and when he put his mouth on me, I shouted.

He licked at the head of my prick, his tongue tracing around the pulled-back foreskin and dipping into the slit to pick up the drops I leaked for him. Pleasure shot up my spine, radiating through me, and I groaned, sinking my hands into his rough-cut hair and begging for more.

Ever the generous lover, Eric gave what I asked. Sealing his lips around me, he sucked, moving all the way down my shaft so his lips reached the base before he swallowed.

The movement of his throat around me set me ablaze, and I thrashed and moaned, doing the most ridiculous dance one could think of as I stood there. When I could take no more without spending, I yanked him away from me, and saw his mouth still moving like a suckling babe's.

"Chrissy. What?"

"I want to taste you as well," I said, sinking down to my knees and pushing him onto his back. I swiveled my hips so that I straddled him, lowering my prick to his mouth, taking his hard shaft in mine.

Lawless moaned, the sound vibrating along my every nerve, and took me in once more. We worked each other relentlessly, our skin beading with sweat, the scent of male passion heady and strong.

My hands found his balls, cupping and rolling them even as my own hips snapped out a rhythm older than ancient Egypt. We rocked and moaned and his fingers slipped between my buttocks and found my hole, before pushing inside. The world went white-hot, my seed shooting out of me like lightning.

Eric spent in my mouth only moments later, his harsh groan echoing the bitter taste of him, the heavy earthiness of his seed.

I toppled over next to him, both of us lying there and breathing hard. He reached out with one hand and grasped my arm, saying nothing. Just letting me know he was there.

It gave me comfort and confidence. With him at my side, I could do anything.

22

———

I found Silad morosely contemplating the mangled earth left by yesterday's inexperienced diggers.

"Not exactly following conventional methods, are they?" I asked him when he turned to me, spreading his hands with deep eloquence.

"They are like afreets, sayyid. Like demons who tear through all they touch."

"I would say so, yes. Why don't we give them the day off? They can mill about and guard nothing. I have a job for you, if you are willing to take it."

"What sort of a job, sayyid?" His eyes, so dark and intelligent, held a knowing look.

"We have been commissioned to find a tomb. We will need help to open it. A member of Professor Zavigny's staff and I have a spot we need to investigate today."

"I see." He stroked his chin, which was still the beardless chin of a young man. "And if I do?"

"You are entitled to anything we find save mummies and sarcophagi."

"This is dangerous work, sayyid. Many things live in dark tombs. You know this, yes?"

My hands clenched, and a chill ran up my spine. I nodded firmly. "Yes. I know."

"Then I will help you. Shall I come now?"

"Yes. Mr. Lawless will meet us at the mouth of the West Valley with the supplies we require."

We took only our hand tools. I trusted Eric to bring the rest, and my trust was not unfounded. He had even managed to procure a donkey.

"Did we need a donkey?" I asked, blinking mildly at him.

"No, but it was this or the trader feller's sister, and I didn't figure we'd have no use for her."

Silad shouted with laughter. "But I might have. Was she pretty?"

"She looked like a mud fence."

"Ah, better the donkey, then."

"You know it."

Silad and Lawless shared a grin, which somehow brightened my own depressed spirits tremendously. Feeling energized, I led the way into the West Valley, feeling as though I knew the path by heart now. I did not need the map, making my way unerringly to the marked fissure in the rock, noting in the light of day how low it really was. When Eric had climbed to it the night before, it had seemed miles above.

Silad shaded his eyes with his hands, staring up. "I can climb up and fasten a rope, sayyid."

"Are you sure? Eric made the climb last night."

He gave me a look of pure scorn. "My people have been climbing these walls since before yours had language."

Eric laughed aloud and clapped Silad on the back. "I like you, Silad. You got balls of solid brass. Go ahead and climb."

Looping the rope over one shoulder, Silad scurried up

the rockface like a lizard, his bare toes finding holds we could not even see from the ground. He was absolutely right. He was completely up to the task.

Crawling up above the tomb entrance, Silad attached the rope to a rocky ledge, jamming stones against the knots to give more security. Then he dropped it down to us.

I grabbed it, but Eric held my wrist, stilling my motion. "I should go first."

His gray eyes met mine, serious and sober now, and I sighed. "If there are inscriptions...."

"Silad can read them. He's up there already. If there's a booby trap, I'll be the one to disable it."

Completely unfair of him to use logic, but there it was. He was right, much as I hated to admit it.

"Very well. Be careful."

"I will." Slinging a pack of tools over his back, Lawless took the rope from me and began to climb.

The wait stretched on interminably, the burning Egyptian sun bringing sweat to my hairline, which ran down into my eyes. I dashed it away impatiently, watching every move Eric made.

He and Silad managed to settle together at the crack in the rock, which in the light of day was clearly large enough to admit a man's body. Silad began to babble excitedly in his own language, and Lawless snorted.

"Speak English, man."

"He says there is a cartouche," I shouted. "Silad, what are the symbols?"

"A throne, an eye and... it is the *shenu* of Osiris!"

"What's that mean?" Eric asked, his voice muffled when he stuck his head into the opening on the rock wall.

"Well, it could mean that Osiris guards this tomb, as he is the guardian of the underworld...." Or, I thought, it could mean that whoever was buried in this tomb was likened so to Osiris that they had named him so.

Certainly *shenu*, or as Napoleon's soldiers had named them, cartouches, often held the names of Osiris or Isis. That was far more common in the Greco-Roman period, however. This tomb might have been from a later period than the newly unearthed dig in the East Valley, but surely it was older than Cleopatra.

"Let me climb up!" I shouted, and both Lawless and Silad's faces popped out over the ledge.

"Not yet," Lawless said. "Let me get this entrance unsealed. There just ain't room enough for all of us to squat up here."

I fairly danced with impatience. The donkey looked at me askance, his ears twitching back and forth while he brayed his opinion on the matter, his square, yellow teeth seeming to mock me. I sighed, drinking a bit of water, because I was sweating bullets, as Eric might say.

Finally Silad appeared once more, grinning a very wide, white grin. "He needs you to send up the large tools, sayyid."

Cursing roundly, I tied the pick and crowbar in the rope and Silad pulled them up, the clanking against the canyon wall making me wince.

"Come *on*," I shouted.

"Hold yer horses, Chrissy. I'm a getting there."

Damn him for laughing at me, I thought. There came a flurry of grunts, groans, and clunking noises, but finally the rope dropped back down.

"Come on, Chrissy. Up."

At last! I climbed, if not gracefully, at least with great speed. The narrow ledge opened to a small, oval opening, just large enough for a man. An ancient man, at that. We would have to wiggle through, especially Lawless, with his strong shoulders.

"You ready, lo—Chrissy?" Eric asked. "Looks like a tunnel."

"I am."

Lawless peered at me through a mask of dust and debris. "You tie that donkey up?"

"Of course I did! Do not treat me like a fool."

He snorted. "We're going in there, honey. We're all fools. Now come on and let's move."

Smart man that he was, Eric had procured a miner's light, which would be most helpful in the enclosed space. He went first, stating that he would be best suited to deal with snakes, scorpions, or large, scaly monsters, making both Silad and I roll our eyes.

Still, the tiny hole with the long, stretching tunnel beyond appeared intimidating enough that I did not argue.

"You next, sayyid," Silad said. "I will guard our back trail."

"Good man." I clapped him on the shoulder in thanks. Really, he had proven over and over that I made a fine choice in hiring him. Taking a deep breath, I went to my knees and crawled inside, only thinking I should have examined the cartouche myself after I was well in.

I followed Eric closely, feeling Silad behind me after only a few moments. Like many of the old tombs, the entry corridor stretched long, nothing before us but inky darkness. I determinedly put my trust in Eric, not allowing myself to think what I might put my hands or my knees upon. Luckily the only thing populating the shaft seemed to be sharp rocks, and though my hands bled, that was far preferable to some poisonous bite.

The air tasted foul, stale, and heavy. Fresh air followed

us in, but by the time Eric stopped before me, I was half-blind and panting, and I ran right into his bum.

"What is it?"

"The whole thing opens up here, but I need to make sure we're not gonna fall off into nothing. Get Silad to pass the lantern up."

The miner's light would only illuminate so far in front of him, best for small spaces and direct contact with the walls. The lantern attached to the pack Silad carried would do much better. Minding the tiny space, I took the lantern and passed it up.

Eric's fingers lingered on mine when they touched. "Thanks, lover," he whispered, and if Silad heard, he made no sign.

"You're welcome. Now tell me what you see."

"Well, it's a big old chamber. There's about a three-foot drop. Here, hold the lamp."

He passed the lantern back to me, and he wiggled about, stirring up a terrific cloud of dust. Sneezing, my eyes watering, I moved to the spot he had just vacated, held up the lantern, and peered about.

"It's the antechamber," I said. "How fascinating."

The chamber appeared to be a natural cavern, which was entirely unusual. It did not possess the uniformity of a cut chamber, the walls flowing in the more circular shape of running water. The walls were not damp, however, so whatever flowing estuary had created this place was gone long before we arrived—indeed, I imagined, before the Egyptians themselves had come.

"Here, come on, Chrissy. I'll help you down."

Lawless eased me down, and Silad followed before we all turned to look at the chamber. Evidence of carvings in the walls, as well as whitewash and colorful paint, were everywhere. In fact, many of the paintings were singularly well preserved.

"Don't touch them!" I said when Eric reached out a hand.

"Huh? Why not?"

"Because the paint will crumble to dust, effendi," Silad said. *Hmph*, I thought. The facts that Silad called me "sir" and that he called Lawless "great man" were not lost on me. Clearly his admiration for Eric's fearlessness equaled mine.

"We might need those paintings to help interpret our next move," I agreed. I started with the wall closest to us, holding the lantern up and peering at the scenes and glyphs.

At first glance they appeared standard enough. Writings from the Book of the Dead. Scenes of the weighing of the soul. Deeds from the great king's life.

It was not until I rounded the first wall that things began to take on a much different cast.

"Silad, come and have a look."

The lines of glyphs began to change here, and even the colors of the paints took on a different tone. Instead of the bright blue of sky and water, the green of oases and the gold of kings, the paintings in this back curve held a darker hue. Almost iridescent, the deep, murky paints seemed to reflect the depths of water and the darkening of the night sky.

"Very strange, sayyid," Silad said, peering closely at a painting of a king in a chariot, his arm upraised, his body turned toward the viewer in the traditional flat manner. The king wore the rounded, upright crown associated with Osiris, but instead of the usual white and gold vestments, the king wore black, a color hardly ever associated with ancient Egypt, except at times in skin color.

"Yes. Look how dark." Accented with a deep bloodred,

the king's suit of bandages seemed out of place. Osiris was often depicted with black skin, but this king was deathly pale in comparison to his clothes, like a photo negative of himself.

The sight disturbed me at first, but the longer I looked, the more it gave me chills.

"What's up, Chrissy?" Eric asked, breaking me out of my reverie.

"Something is askew. Just look at this cartouche."

The usual cartouche for Osiris was a throne with an eye beneath it on the left side, and a king or sphinx-like sitting creature on the right. This cartouche held those images, but it also held another line of figures, each one more monstrous than the next. Even in the simplified form of the Egyptian linear text, I could see claws and tentacles.

"That is.... Sayyid, this is evil. Afreet."

Yes. Demons. They had to be demons of some sort. "Look at this," I exclaimed, following the line of paintings that marched around the next curve of the wall. "It is just like my dreams."

The paintings showed a room, a king on the throne, staring straight ahead. Behind him, hand on his shoulder, stood the black man, the two of them looking like a bizarre yin and yang. The king's face held the expressionless look most Egyptian paintings took on. The dark man, however, betrayed a wide, white smile.

"What's this guy?" Lawless said. "Your boogeyman?"

"I think so, yes."

Silad backed away from us. "Afreets visit you in your dreams, sayyid? This is danger."

"I did warn you, Silad. If you need to go, do so now. We need to know we can depend upon you."

"No. Silad is no coward." He drew himself up, setting his thin shoulders. "It is bad, though. Very bad."

"I know. I agree." I smiled at him, feeling sympathy for his fear. Silad came from a much more superstitious people, so his determination made him seem far more brave than either I or Eric.

"Have we seen all we need to see here?" Eric finally asked, shifting from foot to foot.

I turned in a full circle, looking about. I would need to record a great deal of this, but there seemed little more that I needed to view immediately. The sense of urgency about our errand pushed me on when my academic self would have continued to study.

"Yes, yes. We should move on."

"Well, come on, then."

Forging ahead, Lawless moved to the opening of the next corridor, lighting the way so Silad and I could check for various spells and curses. It never hurt to know what was before us.

There seemed no rhyme or reason to the images that marched down the long corridor, save for the fact that they much more resembled the monstrous paintings on the back wall than the usual spells and writings. Each time we encountered a new creature unknown in traditional mythology, Silad would spit through his fingers to ward off evil.

Really, he was going to be dry as a mummy before we got to the burial chamber.

I blamed the bad air for my slow thinking, but it did strike me once we arrived in the next chamber that very little debris impeded our process. Carter and Carnarvon had been forced to dig through tons of dirt and rock, but this tomb showed no signs of cave-in. Or of tomb robbers.

"Very odd, sayyid," Silad said, echoing my thoughts. "It could have been created only last week."

"What's odd?" Eric asked.

"Well, a tomb this old should have more detritus. Yet the walls are clean, there have been no cave-ins, and there is no water damage to speak of. It is rather pristine."

"Well, that's a good thing, right? Makes it easier for us."

"One hopes," I said, staring around this new room.

"They prepared the body here." Silad pointed to the pots and jars that remained miraculously unharmed. Alabaster and gold, clay and wood, the containers lined the walls. The more ominous tools were there as well, made of bronze, primitive things that looked like modern rib spreaders and scoops for organ removal.

"Oh, that's just wrong," Eric said, staring fixedly at a sharp, poker-like implement.

"They felt they were preserving him for the next life. I am sure you would have wanted them to do a thorough job, had it been you back then."

"Unh-uh. No way. No how."

His vehemence had me chuckling. "No mummy for you, my boy?"

"No siree. What's all this?"

Woven baskets held the scrappy remains of linen wrappings. "This is the leftover material. Look at the sheer gold. Do not even breathe hard on it."

"I won't. I'm not touching. Promise." He gave me a grin, clapping me on the back, which made me wheeze.

"We need to find the burial chamber. Silad, you need to mark in your mind what is here that you might like to take with you."

"Yes, sayyid." Voice low and hushed, Silad stared at the wrappings, some of them spangled with jewels and faience, the brightly painted plaster medium used to decorate beads and tiny statues.

It looked as though the thought of such riches was going a long way to alleviate Silad's fear.

When we reached the next chamber, which was the treasury, we all stopped short, a low moan coming from us collectively. Simply breathtaking.

I had assumed, since pieces of this tomb had been found all over the terrain between the East and West Valleys, that tomb robbers had sacked the place many years before.

Now I felt that perhaps the few missing pieces had been left like breadcrumbs, a trail for us to follow.

The rest of the throne stone leaned against the back wall. Armies of ushabtis in every color of faience marched through the center of the room. Baskets of food, jugs of water, and pots of cosmetics were strewn about as if the man using them had simply gone to bed and would return in the morning to set things right.

"Good God Almighty," Eric breathed.

"Alhamdulillah," Silad agreed. Praise be to God.

"Where do we start?"

"We don't." When Eric looked at me sideways, I shrugged. "We must find the burial chamber."

"Right. We can, uh, look at this shit on the way out, right, Silad?"

Ah, treasure hunters. Not that I was not salivating over some of the items, but....

"What is this, sayyid?"

I crossed the floor carefully, not wishing to crush anything in my clumsiness, to peer at what Silad had found.

"It looks like an altar."

"To who?" Eric came over to stand beside me. "Damn, that's...."

"Yes." Despite the sweltering heat, I shivered. The altar was carved out of the same stone as the throne, an eerie depiction of the night sky. Rather than the angular, pleasing shape of the traditional Egyptian altar to Horus or Osiris, this carving was misshapen, ovoid, with an undulating edge that looked like a page burned out of a book.

On the altar stood more than twenty tiny statues, all carved in black stone, each one more disturbing than the next. Great shaggy beasts, hulking forms with tentacles for beards, and writing masses of eyeballs shared space with less recognizable forms. Only one space lay empty, and when I took the black man with the spiked head out of my bag, it fit perfectly there.

The torches flickered. We all jumped.

"Well. Let's find that burial chamber, huh?"

"Yes. Yes, I think we should."

As one, we turned away from the apparition in black stone and moved toward the only other doorway in the room, all of us silent save for the scrape of our feet over rock.

Cautiously we moved into the final chamber, which seemed to soak up our light, the darkness penetrating right to our bones. My skin rose with goose bumps, a shiver working all the way through me.

The burial chamber was icy-cold.

"Sayyid...."

"Yes."

"Jesus Christ."

No less than six sarcophagi stood about the room. The large one at the center bore the shape of a man, just as one might expect. The others were smaller, their shapes varying crazily like the altar in the other room, all of them carved with inscriptions that were neither glyphs nor hieratic.

"So what do you say, Chrissy?"

"I say we open them no more than one at a time, take that piece out and destroy it, and come back for the next." That way the remains stood no chance of reattaching themselves. A month ago I would have sneered at the very possibility.

Now I knew better.

"That is wise, sayyid."

"Start with the smallest of them, then."

While they worked to lever the lid off the first sarcophagus, I pushed my foot against the dusty floor, looking at the symbols painted there. I followed them, one line to another, until I realized they formed an askew five-pointed star with an eye in the center. Something about that felt familiar, something I had read but could not recall.

"Damn, but this is tighter than a virgin's thighs," Eric said, huffing. "Help us out, honey."

"Of course." I lent my small amount of strength to theirs, helping Silad work the crowbar, and we finally levered the top off. It had to weigh several hundred pounds, and I wondered how we would open the largest one.

The painted coffin beneath was all gesso and gold, but the shape held no trace of humanity. Instead of depicting body parts or human faces, a terrible host of winged creatures flew across it, so perfectly painted that they seemed to move.

"Hurry," I said, a sudden urgency upon me, as if someone had stepped on my grave.

"We're almost there."

What lay in the coffin was a severed limb, carefully wrapped and perfectly preserved. Rust stains covered the fabric, and it took Silad turning away, gagging, for me to realize that it must not be rust but old, decayed blood.

"God Almighty. Let's go burn this thing."

We took the leg, for it was the lower half of a thigh, a calf, and a foot, and all but ran through the tomb, tripping over jars in the treasury, moving like a stampeding herd of cattle, according to Eric. The last thirty feet we crawled, heedless of our knees and hands, and I was the last one out of the hole, the sun blinding me so completely that I did not see the blow coming, did not even see a shadow of the man who landed it.

Then the heavy, blunt object landed on my skull with brute force, and all I saw was black.

23

I woke to the feeling of hard stone beneath my abraded cheek. I admit, at first I thought I was blinded, because I could not see a thing. Then I realized it was only the inky dark of a tomb that no sunlight penetrated.

For long moments I simply panicked, I admit.

Thrashing about, I tried to sit up, only to realize my hands were bound behind my back. How ridiculous, I thought, to tie me up when I was clearly trapped. It made me quite cross. I might have raged.

What finally brought me out of my fugue state was a thump and a moan. It came from off to my right, and I turned that way blindly.

"Eric?"

"Well, hey, Chrissy. You all tied up?"

Lawless's voice sounded as though he was speaking underwater, slurred and slow, and it occurred to me that both he and Silad might be injured. My head ached, but I seemed little worse for wear besides, but they could have fought our attackers, both of them much more alert than I had been on the trip out of the tomb.

"I am," I replied. "I assume you are as well."

"Hog-tied like a branded calf."

It took me precious minutes to figure that out. "Ah. Americans."

"Shit." He snorted. "Now ain't the time for love words, Chrissy. Just get your ass over here and let's get untied."

"Oh, yes, I shall just scoot right over." Damn him. Struggling to my knees, I shuffled in his general direction. "Damnation!"

"Well, stop banging into things!"

"Oh, yes, let me just light my lamp," I snarled. "In case you cannot tell, it is dark."

"Well, follow my voice. You want me to sing to you?" With that he started yodeling some song about a lonesome trail, and I vow, I worried that they might have hit him too hard. Not as hard as I would when I got to him, but hard nonetheless.

"There you are," he said when I literally ran into him. "Gimme some sugar."

"Are you dying? Because I would hate to be in here with a corpse that was not of the ancient variety."

"Nope. I just have a headache the size of Texas, which is pretty big, for you English types. Kiss me, lover. Just so I know you're real."

My lips found his shoulder first, then his throat, and I worked my way up, groping for his mouth. Tasting blood, I exclaimed, but he caught my lips with his and kissed me hungrily, with a desperation that could only be born from the thought that he had lost me. I knew what he felt, for the same feeling swelled in my breast, and I kissed him hard enough to bruise.

We teetered but righted ourselves, breathing heavily.

"Silad?" I asked.

"Far as I know he's alive. May be in here with us."

"I am here, sayyid," Silad said, his voice weak as a new babe's. "Is there water?"

"I don't know. We'll look when we get loose. Are you harmed?"

"Not so much," he said. "My head hurts."

Of course it did. Poor Silad. He had not come into this as we had, knowing all the possibilities. My heart ached for the danger I had put him in, and that more than anything else stiffened my spine and kept me from leaning on Eric any longer.

"Let's try to get undone, shall we?"

"I've undone you before," Eric said softly, chuckling.

The urge to hit him nearly overwhelmed me. "Now is not the time."

"You're cute when you're mad, Chrissy." But he turned obediently and began to scrabble at me with his hands.

I turned as well, and soon enough, my hands came free, Lawless being far more dexterous than I. I rubbed my wrists before turning about again to work at the knots on his wrists, cursing while I struggled.

"Breathe, Chrissy. We got time."

"Would you stop calling me that!"

Taking a deep breath, I went back to work, and he was quite right. It helped.

"There. I believe you are free."

"I am," he said, spinning about to pull me into a breathless, harsh kiss. "Scared me, lover. Thought we were dead."

"I did too. We should see to Silad."

Silad proved easier to locate, thanks to the matches in Eric's pockets. We had been searched, our weapons and tools gone, but when we lit matches, we found a few small oil lanterns and bottles of water, as well as some oil-paper-wrapped, dried-out sandwiches.

"Well. Clearly they mean to keep us alive for the time being," I said. "We're in the treasury."

The only thing missing when I looked about was the strange altar, the black stone monstrosity and its inhabitants gone.

"Isn't that kinda odd for tomb robbers?" Lawless asked.

"I think we're dealing with something far worse than that, Eric," I replied. "Don't you, Silad?"

Silad spit weakly. "Afreets."

"No, I think not. Men. Men who had a very definite ulterior motive in enlisting us to this task."

"You mean old Zaffiggy and Royale?"

"Yes, precisely."

I examined both entrances to the room. They had been blocked, but just under a foot of open space remained at the top of each archway, providing us with air, thick as it was.

"I think they could not find it themselves, and so they used us to find it for them."

"I don't get it. Zaffiggy has years of experience." Lawless moved about, seeming restless and twitchy, for which I really could not blame him.

"Yes, but he had not our... help."

"The dark man and the map. Why d'you suppose he came to us?"

"Perhaps because we did not know what we were after? We had no ulterior motives, at least not until today."

"Hmph."

"No, he may be right," Silad said. "The afreets do this all of the time. They confuse, convince people to do wrong in the name of right."

"That's real comforting, Silad," Eric said, snarling a little.

"Yes, well, I insist we find a way out of here before they come back to do whatever it is they wish to do with us," I said, suiting words to action. I began searching the widely varied cache of treasure for anything that might open a makeshift door.

"Good idea. You think there's guards out there?"

"We must not rule out the possibility."

"Then you and Silad concentrate on the doors. I'll look for weapons."

That suited me perfectly well, except that after what had to be an hour of searching, none of the three of us had come up with anything useful.

"You think this oil would work as a firebomb?" Eric asked, holding up a violently blue pot of balm.

"No. It ought to make you smell less like the donkey, though."

"Ha-ha."

One by one, we ended up sitting on the floor, staring at the walls around us. Silad put his head down on his knees.

"I think I may be sick, effendi," he said. I assumed he was talking to Eric.

"You took quite a bump, son. Get some rest."

Ever obedient, Silad lay down and curled into a ball. His even breathing soon told us he had dropped off, exhausted from our efforts.

I crawled over to Eric, settling at his side, leaning against his strength. "Is it hopeless, then?"

"Nah. We're just tired, having trouble working it out. Whatever they're doing with the tomb, it will take them hours before they're ready to come back for us. We got time."

Resting my head on his shoulder, I smiled. "Promise?"

"You betcha."

How odd that the cocky, brazen attitude I had once abhorred now comforted me. "I think Zavigny means to try and raise the king."

"Raise him how? Like a son?"

Pinching his arm hard, I growled. "Ho-ho. No, I mean he intends to resurrect him."

"Well, we're fine, then. That ain't possible."

"A few weeks ago I would have agreed. What I have seen since...."

"Is just fancy window-dressing. Get some rest, Chrissy."

"Will you wake me when you want me to keep watch?" I had no wish for him to play the martyr.

"I will."

At this point lying to me would be moot, so I decided to trust. Curling close, I rested my head on his thigh and lay down to sleep some, my poor brain too taxed to do any more thinking.

Either we had time or we had none. One way or the other, I would need my strength.

24

———

The king rose from his throne, the shrieks of the fallen sacrifices still ringing through the room. He raised his face toward the sky, his arms coming up, lifted like a benediction. The black man beside him smiled, the teeth very sharp and stained with blood.

"Yes, my king," the black man said, reaching out with one clawed hand to touch the blank-eyed man on the shoulder. "You see now how it can be if you follow me. Your power will know no bounds, and you will never truly die."

The stare the king turned on the black man was already dead. One hand lifted, almost delicately, a bronze knife held in it, stabbing right into the black man's chest. The robed figure dissolved into a thousand writhing, wriggling maggots, the size and rubbery thickness of them sickening to see, even as they escaped through cracks in the floor.

When the black man disappeared, so did the winged serpents, which had flocked about, eating this subject and that. The few remaining sacrifices turned as one and overtook the king, rending him limb from limb, great gouts of blood spewing forth to stain

*the walls and floors with the life force of the man who had taken
their friends, their families, and their lives.*

I woke, gasping, having no sense of where I was or why.

It took long moments to realize that Eric was shaking my
shoulder, pressing tiny kisses against my mouth.

"Wake up, Chrissy," he said over and over. "I can't keep
my eyes open."

Unbending from my uncomfortable position took
precious moments, but I did, reaching for one of the jugs of
water that had been left for us. My mouth felt like the
Sahara in the summer.

"Sorry," I croaked. "Was dreaming."

"Yeah, you were caterwauling."

"Sorry," I repeated. "You may sleep now."

"Thanks, lover. Wake me if you hear something."

Lawless curled up beside me and was asleep almost
immediately. A quick glance told me that Silad still slept,
and his color was not good at all, so I left him that way.
There was no need to wake him when we knew good and
well we would not leave until our hosts came for us.

I gnawed on a crust of dry bread, running the events of
the last few weeks through my mind and wondering how I
had been so stupid as to let myself be used the way I had.
Perhaps it had simply been that collusion between Zavigny
and Royale had seemed so *unlikely.*

The hair rose on the back of my neck, drawing my gaze
up, and I flinched back when I saw the apparition before
me. Wearing the same skin and robes as he had before, the
dark man stood there, but where his head should be, a
single tentacle stood out, vicious and long and sharp.

One overlong arm reached out, a scaly, clawed hand
touching my cheek. "You have served the king well," it said,
though it had no mouth to speak. "You will be rewarded."

And then it was gone, the vision of it fading even as a violent blow reverberated from the door leading to the outer reaches of the tomb. And the exit.

Lawless woke with a start, sitting up so quickly that he hit his head on my chin. My ears ringing and my tongue dripping blood, I tried to right myself, attempting to make myself ready to fight.

Silad popped up like a jack-in-the-box, blinking and scrambling to his hands and knees. I knew we could count on him for assistance, and that we would get no more time for preparation.

A positive flurry of blows landed on the makeshift door, the sound of wood splintering and cracking echoing through the treasury. We all three held our breath, expecting the worst, so what we saw when the door fell shocked us all into utter immobility.

My employer, Mr. Royale, stood in the light cast by the glow of perhaps five lanterns. Five lanterns held by the burly American and European guards the man had employed to protect the dig.

Royale stared from me to Eric to Silad, his face a study in rage, red and puffy, the vein that throbbed in his forehead near to bursting.

"Well, come on, boys," he boomed out, gesturing to us to rise. "We ain't got all night. Best get your asses in gear if you want to get out of here."

25

W e all stared back at him, the bright light from his lanterns blinding us. I cast about for something to say, but it was Eric who found his voice first.

"Well now, no offense, Mr. Royale, but we thought you was in on it."

Not exactly eloquent, but it echoed my sentiments exactly.

Royale let out an explosive sigh, scrubbing one hand over his face. "I signed on for treasure, boys. Not murder. Now, come on and get, or we'll get got."

Without trying to wrap my brain around his sentence structure, I stood, swaying. I hoped I was the picture of outrage.

"You set us up."

"Now, son, just set you up to find shit for me. I had no idea what Zavigny had in mind. I ain't no weird zealot. Will you all come *on!*"

The guards were milling about now, nervously looking down the corridor they had arrived by, and that more than anything got us moving. It took both of us to lift Silad, who had taken the worst of the beating, clearly.

One of the guards gave Silad a few sips of water and then we were off, a pitiful parade if I do say so myself. We limped along, the guards surrounding us, Royale leading the way. He muttered to himself the whole while about crazy bastards who ruined things for everyone.

I dreaded making it to the antechamber, for that crawl through the last corridor would be nearly impossible, especially with Silad. Bless his heart.

The power of positive thinking was not on my side. I should have tried harder, for when we spilled out into the huge antechamber, Zavigny was there, alone, a heavy black gun pointing in our direction.

The guards stopped dead, then spread out, fanning along the wall and creating a moving target. The gun in Zavigny's hand never wavered. It pointed straight at me.

"Ah. Well, we shall have to start earlier than I planned, hmm?" Zavigny said with a pleasant smile that sent a cold chill down my spine.

"You son of a bitch!" Eric fairly roared, charging at the professor, pure rage written on his face.

Zavigny shot him. Point-blank. At first I feared the worst, that Eric was shot in the chest, but when he spun in a circle, clutching his upper arm, I knew at least he might live.

"Stop!" I shouted. "Just stop. What do you want from us?"

Watching Eric like one might watch a worm dangling from a hook, Zavigny waved the gun. "I want you to stop the heroics, if you will."

I went to Eric, mindful of the gun. His arm had no more than a graze, but in this dusty, ancient environment, it needed to be dressed. I took the handkerchief I knew was in his pocket and wrapped it about the wound, ignoring his oath.

"How touching," Zavigny said. "And how pointless. But then, I need all the blood I can get."

"Look, Frenchie," Royale began. "You don't want to do this. It ain't gonna work."

The pleasant smile left Zavigny's face, replaced by a feral snarl. "It will, and I will rule at his side."

"Whose?" I asked.

"The king. Osiris. Surely you know that now, my dear."

"You can't mean to raise him from the dead! Do you have any idea how many people will die?" I demanded.

His eyes took on the glow of true zeal. "He is the true king of Egypt! He will return the glory to this place."

"You're insane, Zavigny. Rush him, boys!" Royale charged, much as Eric had, and Eric pulled me down on the floor, flat as a pancake.

Instead of the fiery blaze of guns, however, a cloud of black smoke descended upon Royale and his guards, blinding them, becoming an oily curtain between Zavigny and the men.

The shadows began to take forms, giant creatures dropping out of them, twisting, writhing snakelike bodies with heads like blind birds. One of them latched on to Royale's leg, ripping it clean away, blood spurting in great gouts as Royale screamed.

I could hear Silad gagging, but Eric just crawled back toward the corridor that led to the treasury and the burial chamber, cursing with every breath. Silad followed, his eyes rolling with terror as a great, rough-skinned creature with fifty tentacles for a face formed from the inky black mist and grabbed two of the guards in its clawed hands.

"Save the three for me!" Zavigny shouted.

Which is where we began, wasn't it? Two of the guards disappeared into the gaping maw of the beast. Royale was nothing but scraps. And Eric was pulling me back into the ground, deeper and deeper into the tunnel that led back to our prison.

Back where Zavigny no doubt wanted us to go.

"Goddamned crazy son of a bitch," Lawless was saying, grunting every time his arm slammed against rock. "We got to get somewhere we can barricade up."

"Did you see...?" Silad babbled, his breath coming in sobs. "Afreets, effendi. All afreets."

"I saw." Eric yanked me around the corner into the treasury, moving Silad back so he could start piling detritus in front of the arch. "I saw every damned bit."

We could still hear wet, gurgling screams.

God in heaven, I thought. *Help us.*

"That's not gonna hold it. We need—Jesus fuck!"

Eric's exclamation had me spinning about to see the dark man from the market, the one from my dreams. He spread his arms, grinning with a full set of crocodile teeth, his hands enormously disproportionate claws.

"My friends!" he cried, his voice echoing crazily throughout the room like an explosion underwater. "You have come to free the king! Welcome."

His voice reverberated in my head, making my eyes roll back in my head. Silad fainted dead away. Eric cried out, dropping my arm to put his hands to his ears, and I fought to stay on my feet as long as I could, finally falling to the floor in a convulsion. Until once again the world went black.

26

The sound of chanting rang across stone, almost like the scrape of a sword on bone. I thought for a moment that I was dreaming, as I had so often. Where else would I expect to open my eyes and see men dressed like ancient Egyptian priests, kneeling on the floor and speaking arcane languages?

Soon enough I realized I was chained to the wall, my weight dragging on my arms, making my shoulders twist up on themselves. My head rested on one arm, and my face felt hot and swollen. I must have hit hard when I fell.

It had the unreality of an elaborate school prank. I spent a good many minutes simply staring at the tableau. When I opened my mouth to scoff at myself, to tell myself to wake up, no sound came out. Just a dry croak.

When I tried to turn my head, my vision blurred, so I had no idea if Silad and Eric still lived. The very thought gave me a terrible pang in my chest.

Zavigny lived, for he stood in the center of the circle of chanting men (I could not bring myself to call them priests), dressed in the kilt and crown of a pharaoh—a ridiculous costume for him, with his pasty skin and sagging chest. He raised his arms, holding what looked like a forearm in his hands.

I swallowed my gorge and tried once more to lift my head, this time managing to see Lawless to my left. He hung lifeless in his chains, but his chest rose and fell, so I felt as though it might be worth setting my mind to trying to find a way out of there.

While I tried to cudgel my brain into working, Zavigny intoned loudly and placed the piece of mummy he held on the great stone slab that had held the largest sarcophagus. We were in the burial chamber. That notion at least told me my mind was clearing.

The nightmarish scene went on, Zavigny reassembling the king, piece by piece. He shouted triumphantly when he placed the head, stepping back and reciting some unintelligible incantation, and the priests all paused expectantly.

Nothing happened.

"No! Something is wrong! Something is missing. What is it?" Turning in a circle, Zavigny cast about, his eyes flaring wildly. When they fixed on me, they evinced pure hatred.

"What have you done? What did you take?"

The sound of Eric clearing his throat scraped across my nerves. I turned just in time to see him spit blood.

"He didn't, you little toad. I did. You're missing a toe, I think."

"What? How... you bastard, you will tell me where it is."

I should have been watching Zavigny, but Eric's wide, horribly bloody smile riveted me. He laughed, the sound sharp and bright.

"No, I don't think so, you crazy sumbitch."

"Search him!"

How Eric had known to remove a piece of the dead king,

I do not know. I suppose it stood to reason, but I had never even thought of it. How I admired him then, as Zavigny's men came to rifle through Eric's torn clothing.

"It's not here, sir."

"What have you done with it?" Zavigny's voice rose to a shriek. "What have you done?"

"Maybe I dropped it outside," Eric answered. "With any luck a wild dog is gnawing on it."

Spittle dripped from the corner of Zavigny's mouth, and his eyes narrowed ominously. "I don't believe you. Jacques, unlock young Christian."

One of the priestlike fools came over and unchained me, catching me when I fell, my whole body lighting up with white-hot agony as my limbs came back to life. Zavigny strode over to me, his bony knees making me laugh out loud, a sound that ended abruptly when he gave me a ringing slap.

"Where is it?"

"I do not know," I said. "I didn't know he took it."

"*Merde.* You think you can fool me, Christian? I have bested you at every turn. Now tell me!" He hit me again, just for emphasis, I thought.

"He don't know! Just quit it." Eric shifted, his chains jangling.

"Well, perhaps you will tell me to save him, hmm?" Pulling a bronze dagger out of the garter that held up his wool socks, Zavigny held it to my throat. "Tell me or I kill him now."

"I'd rather watch you slit his throat than watch him get eaten by something later." Those clear gray eyes, even with the skin swollen around them, burned into me, as sober as an executioner's.

I understood. I felt the same. Better a quick death for him than watching him suffer.

I loved him so in that moment that I ached.

"You will not fool me," Zavigny cried. "I have seen the two of you together, in your perverse little love affair." The knife point moved from my throat to my eye. "Tell me or he will die in slow degrees."

I could see the flare of fear in Eric's eyes, and I would have shaken my head at him, telling him not to give in, but the knife hovered, and my eye fluttered shut.

"No. You sumbitch. I ain't gonna."

The knife dragged down my cheek, a trail of fire sparking in its wake. I tried not to scream, but a cry escaped me despite my best efforts.

"You're crazy," Eric shouted. "Jesus Christ."

"Tell me." Now the knife pressed right against my tear duct, and I stood there and shook, waiting for Zavigny to gouge my eye out.

"All right! All right. It's in the treasury."

"The exact location?"

Eric grunted, one of the guards poking him in the ribs. "I don't know. I threw it back behind the chariot."

"Then Christian and I will go and look for it, hmm?" Prodding me once more with the knife, Zavigny forced me to rise. I saw the agonized look on Eric's face as we were separated.

I agreed wholeheartedly.

Bringing along two guards to light the way, Zavigny pushed me out of the burial chamber and into the treasury. "On your knees, Christian. Look carefully."

At his shove, I fell to the floor and began to crawl, ostensibly looking for the missing toe. What I was really looking for was a weapon, of course, and I blessed Eric again for giving me the opportunity. There were alabaster pots and bronze bowls, but none of them would help me against Zavigny *and* the guards, so I kept looking.

Crawling between the stacks of food and drink, I kept my head down, speaking almost casually. "You're quite mad, you know. I have seen in my dreams what happens when the king rises. He will kill you."

"He will not! His emissary has promised me all of the riches and all of the recognition I deserve."

"Emissary," I scoffed, glancing at him over my shoulder. "You mean the dark man. He is not your friend."

"He is my right hand! He is the one who led me to you. He said you would find the tomb, and so you did."

I wondered, as I crawled there on my knees, why me? What was it about me that the dark man wanted? Why had he not given Zavigny the map?

"Yes, and I did, didn't I? More fool I," I complained bitterly.

"You were brilliant, my boy." His foot prodded my arse. "Get looking."

The staff I found was far too brittle to use as a weapon. So were the arrows. I began to despair. Surely there had to be something... ah. A papyrus case. Made of smooth, dark stone with a leather-hinged lid, it was perfect. I put my hand on it when I moved forward, gripping it hard.

"I think I may have it."

Eager, just as I knew he would be, Zavigny crowded in behind me, leaning down to look.

I brought the box up and back, smashing him in the face with the lid as hard as I could.

He screamed, the sound one of pure rage, and I scrambled away, trying to keep out of arm's reach. The guards stumbled forward, realizing all was not well, but I managed to slip behind the remains of the chariot, only then realizing that the damned toe was exactly where Eric said it was.

Scooping it up, I stuffed it in my pocket and made for the door, leaping one guard and whacking at the other with the box I held. I would have made good my escape but for one impediment.

The dark man appeared at the door the instant I would have rushed through, blocking my way. While Zavigny closed in on me from behind, the man held out a clawed appendage, palm up, waiting for me to hand over the missing piece.

With Zavigny's bronze knife poking at my back just above my kidneys, I handed it over.

27

When Zavigny led me back into the room, Eric's face fell. I could not blame him. He'd thought, no doubt, that I would win free and come back with help. Had he been in my situation, he would have done so.

"I'm sorry," I said when I passed him.

"Don't be," he returned. "You tried."

I had not seen Silad before, but there he was on the other side of Eric, his head rolling from side to side. Deep, guttural sounds issued from him, each one more hair-raising than the last. There would be no help from that quarter at all.

"Now we have all of the pieces." Zavigny turned to the dark man. "Would you like to put it in place?"

Shaking his malformed head, the dark man gestured for Zavigny to take the piece of mummy and put it where it belonged at the end of the wizened foot.

Something stirred in the chamber when the last piece fell into place. Something foul and dark, like an oily cloud.

The very air thrummed with power, the electricity of it pounding through me, raising the hair on my neck.

Unnoticed now, I moved to Eric's side, my hands tugging at his chains. "It's working," I murmured. "The spell is working."

"No shit, lover. Get me loose before that thing comes to life, will you?"

His chains were held in place by a simple pin mechanism, and I unlocked them, pulling him down into my arms.

"This ain't no time for canoodling," he said as the rock slab began to vibrate in the center of the room. "We got to get out of here."

"But Silad—"

"Don't worry, I ain't leaving him."

The whole focus of the guards or priests or whatever they were was on the mummy, so we freed Silad and carried him toward the door of the chamber. We never managed to make it out, though, for a shock ran through the entire floor of the cavern, and the room began to glow with an eerie green light, a truly phosphorescent light.

We staggered, trying to right ourselves, but Silad's dead weight unbalanced us, and we fell, landing hard on the stone. An unearthly wail filled our ears, an entirely inhuman sound, and the dark man spread his arms, shouting in that freakishly loud voice.

"My king! You have returned to the land of the living."

28

Several things happened simultaneously. Silad began to wake. Lawless's arm began to bleed once more. And the king began to move.

Horrific, shambling like a great bear, the king rose off the slab he lay on, moving toward the reassembled throne.

"We have to stop him."

Eric glared at me. "Well, no shit. But what do we do?"

"I don't know." Without waiting for him to answer, I threw myself at the king, grabbing one bandage-wrapped leg. The feel of it made me gag, with its crusted wrappings pulsing with life underneath.

I dimly heard Eric curse and scramble after me, and he lent his strength to mine, his hands clamping on the other ankle and pulling.

The king ignored us, his empty eye sockets focused straight ahead as he lumbered toward his seat of power. The dark man and Zavigny, however, set upon us, trying to pry us off the king. It would have been comical if not for the beating of wings we heard overhead, and the screaming of one of the priests as he was devoured by a beast that dwarfed us and yet somehow still fit under the ceiling of the chamber.

Silad was screaming prayers, and his voice never stopped, unlike the priests'. They shouted and their sounds cut off with wet gurgles, until suddenly it was only Silad and Zavigny who shouted.

Eric and I were grimly silent.

"Kill them!" Zavigny cried. "Kill them now!"

Eric screamed, the sound one of rage rather than pain, then disappeared from my side. A huge, shaggy dog-beast had his leg, pulling on it like a feral dog would pull at a bone, and I knew I should try to contain the king, but I could not watch him die. I simply could not.

I bounced up like a jack-in-the-box, pouncing on the dog's back and beating at its head with my hands. The thing was twice the size of a man, and I feared Eric would simply break in two. My distraction worked, the creature letting Eric go to snap at me, and he crawled away, blood trailing from his leg.

Poor boy, he was having a very bad day.

Pieces of the priests impeded my progress when I let go of the dog thing and scrambled back for the king.

Eric and I reached him just as he sat down on the throne.

Silence descended, the same eerie green glow filling the room, all the monsters disappearing like smoke save for the dark man and Zavigny.

We knelt at his feet like supplicants, staring at the king as the wrappings fell away and flesh began to reassert itself on his form. I could not tear my eyes away, even though the sight nearly sent me into convulsions. I clung to the last shreds of my sanity, thinking only of Eric, I admit.

I wanted him to live.

The face filled in last, and it had the terrible beauty of an ancient Egyptian statue. Cold and lifeless, the face hardly moved, the eyes still empty holes but filled with green light. One hand raised, the fingers pointing directly at Zavigny, who stumbled forward, his hands flying to his throat as if he were choking.

As indeed he was. His face went purple when the king's hand closed about his neck, squeezing the life from him. The king shifted, seemingly casual, and Zavigny rose in the air, his feet kicking, his arms flailing.

He was going to die, and I could not look away. I wanted to see how my own end would come.

The king's lips pulled back from yellowed teeth, and the muscles newly formed in his arm bulged. Zavigny's neck snapped like a twig, and the man flopped like a rag doll.

"Jesus," Lawless breathed.

I quite agreed.

Tossing Zavigny aside, the king held up his hand once more and a long bronze sword appeared in it. My moment seemed at hand, and I bowed my head, waiting for it to be separated from my neck.

"Yes, my king!" came the insane voice of the dark man. "Kill them and we shall rule forever."

I waited for the end, but instead of decapitation, I heard a voice in my head. *"Help me."*

It made my head rock back on my neck, and my eyes flew open just in time to see the sword drive deep into the dark man's body. The scream made me shake, made my hands clasp my head to keep it from exploding.

The dark man seemed to swell like a black cloud, inky drops of blood raining down to stain the dark floor. Each drop became a snake, weaving back and forth, hissing through sharp fangs.

Help the king? How, when I could not even help myself?

Eric cursed, kicking out at a snake and sending it flying. "Goddamn it, Christian, get off your ass and *do* something. Silad, quit your whining and *move*."

Suiting his actions to words, Eric got up and grabbed the sword right out of the king's hand, twirling in circles to behead the snakes. Blood ran from his wounds, and his face screwed up in a grimace of pain, but he was never so magnificent to me.

"Help me." The words came again in my head, causing me to retch from the echo.

"How?" I shouted it, and Eric gave me the strangest look.

The black man had all but dissolved, great tentacles rising from the scorched spot on the floor, perhaps ten of them, all as big around as my body. One of the tentacles wrapped around Silad, and Eric hacked at it, cutting it away and shoving Silad behind him.

"Destroy the altar. Invoke my wife."

Stupidly I stared at the king. What would his wife... in mythology the wife of Osiris was Isis, who had knit him back together after Set destroyed him. But he was already mended.

"Eric! The altar! Destroy the statues."

Zavigny's body was still warm when I rifled over it for the great knife he'd held. There! I stabbed out at the tentacle that had attached itself to my ankle, hacking at the needle-like barbs that sank into my flesh.

Eric rose with a roar, running toward the altar and its little statues, only to fall when a great clawed hand rose from the center of the remains of the dark man and grabbed him.

It was Silad who saved him then. Screeching like a banshee, Silad rushed in and pounded at the thing with a rock, freeing Eric and getting thrown through the air for his trouble. He landed hard against the back wall of the chamber, slumping to the ground.

Each one of the little statues fell to Eric's sword, the black stone shattering like glass. We fought every incarnation of the dark man, from the tentacles to the hands to the snakes, me at Eric's back, letting him do his work. And all the while I racked my brain on how to invoke Isis.

Somewhere, in the back of the academic part of my mind, I remembered that after Osiris's death, Horus had brought Set to Isis, and she had beheaded him.

Yes. She would defeat the dark man. But how?

"Call to her!"

I screamed as the voice invaded my head again, going to my knees.

"Chrissy!" Lawless nearly tripped over me when he stepped back to swing again. "Get up!"

I rose. My knees shook, my leg throbbed where the damned creature had damaged it, and I thought I might simply expire right there. Only the thought of saving Eric kept me going, and I don't mind saying those moments were the most selfless of my life.

Drawing on some childhood memory of Budge's Book of the Dead, I raised my arms and began to chant.

"This ain't no time to get religion, Chrissy," Eric shouted, panting hard, his arm muscles bulging. "I need help."

Help is on the way, I thought at him as hard as I could. Whether or not he could hear me, I never knew. It took all my concentration to remember the prayer of Isis.

"Come, Isis, the protector of us!" I shouted. "Come to us as the wind and heal thy husband so he is whole, and mighty before all the gods! Let our enemies fall beneath thy feet!"

Had I mangled it too badly to work?

Seconds later I had my answer, as a fierce wind began when Lawless destroyed the last of the grotesque statues on the altar. Like a storm at sea, the wind whipped around us, sending the monstrous, grasping appendages that clawed at us spinning away. The power of it whipped me backward so I landed on my arse, shaking me all the way to my teeth.

Eric landed against me, his arms going around me as the wind seemed to coalesce into a blinding golden light, the form of a voluptuous woman wearing a crown of horns shimmering in the eye of the storm.

Opposite her, on the other side of the king, the black cloud staining the floor rose up into the form of the dark man once more, this time with no robe. His head bore a shock of bloodred hair.

The Isis figure raised a finger, pointing at the dark man. "You will not win the day."

"He is mine!"

I found myself laughing hysterically, but Eric slapped me, bringing me back around.

"What do we do, Chrissy?"

"The sword," I finally managed to gasp out. "Give her the sword."

Lawless rolled like a man thrown from a horse, landing at the queen's feet, the sword offered up like a last-ditch prayer.

What happened then can only be described as a clash of titans. Isis flew at the dark man, whom I refused to call Set, and swung the sword with terrible strength. The Set figure held up his arms to stop her, but the sword sliced through them like melted butter, severing the arms and the head at the neck. A shockwave hit me and lifted me like a wave on the ocean, sending me reeling back, clutching at Lawless when he fell on me.

The quiet that descended rang with death.

I could hardly fathom that I was still alive.

"Help me, my wife." The king's lips never moved, but this time I knew Eric heard it as well, for he put his hands to his ears.

"Yes, my king. I shall help you. At last."

Multicolored wings fanned out on her back, just as I had read about as a child. Isis enfolded the king in them, the ends fanning out enough to move. While we watched, they shared a kiss, one that nearly broke my heart.

Then the green light in the king's eyes faded, and his skin began to shrivel. He simply fell to pieces, his body disintegrating back into the shattered mummy he had been before Zavigny and company had brought him back.

Crystal tears fell from the queen's eyes when she turned them on us. "Burn his body. Destroy the tomb. He must never live again."

Then, with only the tiniest breeze, she was gone.

29

———————

"What in hell just happened?" Lawless asked me.

"I'll tell you," I said through stiff lips. "But let's get out of here first."

I felt that all of Zavigny's men must be dead, so we were safe in leaving the remains in the tomb for now. Eric did take that toe, though. Just in case.

We dragged ourselves out of the burial chamber, hauling Silad with us, making our way to the main corridor with considerable difficulty. By this time our need for water and medical attention drove us on, though, no matter how I dreaded finding the end of the narrow tunnel blocked. Eric went first, despite my protestation that he was injured.

"Blocked," he said, his voice echoing. Still, it sounded nothing like the horrors we'd faced, so I simply sighed.

"We'll just have to unblock it, then."

"Right. I'll put that order in. One blocked door, open."

The urge to hit him overwhelmed me. Luckily he was out of range. He slipped back down the tunnel toward us, very nearly reaching us before a terrific explosion sounded at the tomb's entrance, flattening Eric as he shot out of the tunnel.

Light streamed in, the flickering of many lanterns reaching us all at the same time.

I feared the worst. *Who knew Zavigny had so many men?* I thought, searching the antechamber for someplace to hide and finding none. The three of us stood side by side, ready to face whatever evil was upon us.

The first head to poke out of the tunnel was a familiar one, but not someone I would ever expect to do evil. It was my mother's relation, Marion.

He surveyed us with a jaundiced eye. Finally he spoke. "Well, Christian, you always were a handful. What on earth have you gotten yourself into now?"

I laughed, long and hard. It seemed the only thing to do under the circumstances.

30

"No," I told the Director of Antiquities firmly, "we must destroy the tomb completely."

Lacau looked from Marion to me and back again. "But think of the knowledge that will be lost!"

We had been in his office for nearly an hour—me, Lawless, Marion, all of us discussing what had occurred. Poor Silad had been hospitalized. The trauma of the experience had damaged him, though the doctors expected a full recovery with time and care.

"Chrissy's right," Lawless said. "That place ain't nothing but trouble."

"And the history is so tainted by generations of cult use that it is not worthy of study," Marion agreed. "Surely you must see that, Pierre."

Lacau seemed unconvinced but finally agreed. "Very well. But I expect you to do it yourselves. I must maintain deniability."

"Of course, of course," Marion said, standing and clapping his hands jovially. "We'll take a small expedition party tomorrow. Come on, lads. You need your rest."

Glad to have the ordeal of the interview over, I rose with alacrity. Lawless followed more slowly, for while he was certainly not permanently damaged, he was stiff and sore and covered with bites, scrapes, and gunshots.

Marion waylaid me just outside. "You go on, Eric, my boy," he said. "I need Christian for just a moment."

With a dubious look, Eric went to wait for me at the front of the building.

"You knew what Zavigny was up to, didn't you?"

Marion raised his brows. "No indeed. I knew Royale was trading in illegal antiquities. And I knew that he and Zavigny had some connection to each other and to an unfound tomb. Word does get around."

"Why didn't you give me more warning?" I could not work up much ire. I had gotten myself into the mess with the professor and Royale and luckily had come out alive. With Eric.

"I couldn't be sure.... Ah, well. And to be truthful, I was more worried about you and your young man. You will be careful, won't you?"

"Of course I will. You won't tell my mother?"

"No. I will leave that to you. Shall we meet in the morning? Say nine?"

"Make it ten. We will be at the Winter Palace."

"Good lad. I shall see you tomorrow, then."

I had no desire to go back to the tomb, but Eric and I both felt we owed it to whatever force had saved us, whether it was the wind or the spirit of Isis.

Joining Eric, I put a hand under his elbow to help him into our waiting car. The Ministry of Antiquities had supplied it for us, a very decent thing, I thought.

"Are you ready to go back to the hotel and rest, love?"

"You know it, lover. I swear to God, next time I get a job

and people tell me my boss is crazy right off the bat? I'm a'quittin'."

"Oh yes. I think that is a very wise idea indeed."

The ride back to the hotel took only minutes, and when we arrived, Eric indulged in ordering us a bath. Marion had insisted upon taking us to the hospital, so we were relatively clean, but we needed a good long soak to ease our bones.

Once we were settled in the big copper tub, me with my back to Lawless, he with his arms around me, he asked what he had wanted to know before.

"So tell me what all that was about, Chrissy?"

"I can only conjecture," I said. "Mythology says that Osiris was the King of All Egypt. In the myth, his brother Set kills him, hacks him into bits, and scatters him. His queen, Isis, knits him back together, and from there he becomes a god, the ruler of the underworld."

"Yeah, well, our boy Zavigny seems to have gotten it all wrong, then."

"Perhaps it was the myth that was distorted."

Lawless stroked my belly. I found it extremely distracting.

"What do you mean?" he asked.

"Well, what if the king was under the influence of a magician? A dark monster like our black man? If he were the source of the magician's power, causing the destruction of his people, he might find a way to end it."

"But in all your dreams, he was willing...."

"No. In all of my dreams, he merely sat and did nothing. This time he fought back."

"Huh. So you think that really was Osiris?"

"I think he was certainly the base for the myth."

"We got to destroy that tomb, Chrissy."

"And we will. Tomorrow. For tonight...." I turned in his

arms, careful of his injuries and the bubbles that surrounded us. "Kiss me?"

I had asked that once before, feeling quite the fool. Now I felt it was my due.

Smiling, Lawless bent to set his mouth to mine, his hands coming up to hold my head. His thumbs traced my cheeks even as his tongue opened my lips to push inside and taste me.

Arching into him, I spread my legs, letting my prick grow and expand against his thigh. My ankle must have hit one of his scrapes, because he grunted, pushing me away briefly, panting a little.

"Sorry," I said, stroking his cheek.

"No. No apologies. I'm fine." Those gray eyes stared into mine, and I smiled, for the look in them was so hungry, so needy, that I could not argue with him.

"We'll simply have to be careful." Mindful now, I kissed him again and again, both of us floating in the water a bit, his hands on my arse holding me in place. He squeezed and pressed and my cock met his, making me buck.

Water splashed out on the floor, and I realized it had gone tepid. "Come on, love. Let's get to bed where we can do this properly."

"Always so proper, my Chrissy." Laughing, he heaved me up out of the water, then stood so we could rinse off.

Bruises bloomed across his skin, and he had a bandage on his arm, one I would have to attend to later. Both of us had tiny marks on our legs in rows of three and four where the monstrous tentacles had found us, but none of those looked putrid, so we chose to ignore them.

We rinsed off slowly, touching each other as though each kiss and stroke was a rediscovery. Perhaps it was; we were irrevocably changed by our experiences together.

When we stepped out of the tub and went to the bed, we walked hand in hand.

I pushed Eric down on his back, mindful of bruises and sore muscles, and spread his legs with my hands. Beautifully hard for me, his prick bobbed against his belly, the skin at the head already pulling back.

Grasping his cock in my hand, I bent to kiss at the tip, licking away the drops there, a moan escaping me at the flavor of him. I moved from his prick to his belly, teasing him with light touches of my mouth, my chin bumping his prick with every move.

"Making me crazy, lover."

"That's the idea," I murmured, moving down to his thighs. He tasted of soap, the springy hairs still damp, and I nuzzled my cheek against the tender skin of the inside of his leg, laughing when he twitched and chuckled.

I worked down to the sweet spot behind his knee before moving back up to his balls, the heavy sacs pulled up tight for me. Pushing them with the flat of my tongue gained me a deep groan, and Eric's hands fell hard on my shoulders, squeezing and stroking.

So soft, the skin there, wrinkled and fuzzy, and I mouthed him gently, my hand closing about the base of his cock.

"Christian! Jesus, come on."

Smiling, I gave him what he needed, rising up and taking his prick in my mouth, sealing my lips about him and sucking hard. As if that were all the permission he required, he began driving into me, his hips rocking up and down. Thick, ridged flesh filled my mouth and my throat, and I closed my eyes and let him take me, relaxing as best I could.

He stroked my hair back off my forehead, cupped the back of my head in his hands, and thrust fast and hard. I could feel how close he was in the quivering muscles of his belly, in the hardness of his thighs, and I simply worked to get more of him in my mouth.

His cry erased whole hours of screams and pain from my memory, sharp and deep, a hoarse approximation of my name. His seed filled my mouth and throat and I swallowed him down, savoring him, savoring the knowledge that I had given him such pleasure.

Licking my lips, I pulled off him, smiling and stroking his belly while he blinked up at me, cheeks flushed a deep red.

"Your turn," he said, and before I could blink, I lay on my back, my hands fisted in the sheets while he put his mouth on me.

The pleasure was immediate and immense, making me cry out. I had not even realized I was so hard, so desperate. Lawless did not tease me as I had him. He simply loved me, his lips riding up and down my cock, his tongue working me the whole way.

I lasted perhaps a minute. Perhaps less. I spent so hard that my vision clouded, my hips spanking the air as I thrust and thrust, giving Eric all I had.

We curled together when he crawled up next to me, both of us exhausted by the events of the last days, and holding to each other, we slept.

31

———————

The king sat on a throne of gilded wood, the arms curling under his hands, the lion heads beneath them shining with jewels. His queen sat beside him, her horned crown gleaming in the light. His hand rested atop hers.

The king had a smile on his face. No longer did he stare straight ahead, stoic and half-dead.

"I knew you would save us," I heard in my head. "I knew I chose well."

And then the image faded, leaving me staring into the dark hotel room, my heart pounding in my chest.

The Egyptians had believed in the unification of the soul with the gods. I supposed that both the good and the bad of them had seen something in me that I never had.

I turned to Eric, needing his touch, and he woke at the first stroke of my fingers on his face.

"Bad dream, Chrissy?"

"No. A good one, if you would believe. I need you."

Sliding across the cotton sheets, he touched me, his hands running up and down my arms. "You got me. I'm right here."

"Good." Pushing him back down, I moved to straddle his thighs, my hands curling around his cock. I stroked him to full hardness, needing him inside me so badly that I did not wish to waste any time.

"Christian. Damn, lover."

"Yes."

Pushing two of my fingers into my mouth, I wet them thoroughly so I could reach back and open myself for him. He moaned, his fingers tracing my sternum, then moving to pluck at my nipples, making me buck for him.

I stretched myself quickly, uncaring of the burn, and soon enough I was ready for him. Moving back, I bent to suck him into my mouth, wetting his prick as well. I could not wait the endless minutes it would take to find the oil.

Rising above him, I settled his cock at my entrance, feeling the broad head push at me. I stared down at him as I pushed myself onto his prick, my hands sliding down his arms to hold his hands.

"Ready, love?"

"God, yes."

So was I. I began to move upon him, sliding up and down his length, feeling him burn inside me. He stretched me almost unbearably, but that was exactly what I craved, what I needed to make me forget.

I laughed out loud, the feeling so huge, so intense.

"No laughing at me in bed, lover," Eric said, but his teeth flashed white in a broad smile. He grasped my cock, stroking it in time with my movements, and I leaned back, my hands on his thighs, really finding a rhythm.

We rocked together, growing wilder and hotter, and my cock throbbed in his hand. I wasn't willing to let go so soon, though, so I gritted my teeth and kept on, denying myself the ultimate pleasure for as long as I could.

Lawless thrashed under me, his every breath a grunt, his hips smacking up against me. I loved the way his muscles stood out under his skin, the way his other hand went to my hip to speed me on, his whole body begging for release.

In the end, it was Eric who could not hold on any longer, and he spent himself deep in my body, his wet heat flooding my senses.

I came with a harsh cry, shaking, my cock throbbing with seemingly endless spasms. I coated his hand and belly with my seed, the scent of us so strong and good that it made me moan and twitch, my spent prick trying to strive for more.

Collapsing against him, I kissed his throat, unable to believe how much my opinion of him had changed.

"You're still a barbarous American, you know."

"And you're still a prissy Englishman." He stroked my back, fingers tracing along my spine. "Good thing I love you too much to care, Chrissy."

"Oh. Yes. That's a very good thing indeed." I smiled, filled to bursting with love for him. "And don't call me Chrissy."

32

———————

We broke our fast with Marion, both of us sore and stiff. Judicious application of strong Turkish coffee and some lovely pastries went a long way toward improving my mood, however.

Lawless was fully outfitted once more, his hat and duster hanging on the back of his chair, his guns in plain view. Whether someone had returned his own weapons or he had acquired more I did not know, but he seemed much more relaxed wearing his cowboy trappings.

Marion simply raised a brow upon seeing them. "Are we going to war, son?"

Lawless gave Marion an ironic look. "Well, it sure pays to be prepared around here."

"True. True."

What had seemed an endless walk to the tomb of the god king felt much shorter on donkeyback, and it occurred to me then to enquire about our donkey from the last trip.

Marion looked at me strangely but assured me that the animal was just fine.

We crawled into the tomb far more carefully than we

had the last time, all of us wary of any strange beings or more prosaic dangers, such as snakes or tomb robbers.

"Oh. What a shame to have to destroy it," Marion said when he saw the interior chambers. "So beautiful."

"Sure, if you can ignore the bloodstains," Eric drawled, at his most offensive.

"Oh. Yes. Quite."

Clearly the Director General had sent a crew to work, for most of the gore was cleaned. How entertaining was the thought that the Antiquities Department had a cleaning crew? We made our way to the burial chamber, and that room was still... well, at least Zavigny's body was gone.

The king's body still lay in pieces, and we gathered them up to take them out into the light. I felt as though I knew him, now, and it was like having a funeral for a friend.

A brazier had been set up down below the mouth of the tomb, and as we lit the pieces of the king afire, I stared into the flames, at once sad and relieved.

"Thy god giveth existence," I murmured. "The god judgeth the truth. Give thyself to the god, guard thyself well for the god daily, and let tomorrow be as today."

"What?" Eric asked, his hand grazing mine.

"Just some half-remembered prayer from the Book of the Dead. It seemed appropriate."

The last piece to go in the fire was the toe Lawless had carried out of the tomb, just in case. Watching it burn, I felt like the god king might now rest in peace.

"So, what now, Chrissy? Not going to run from me again, are you? 'Cause that might piss me right off."

"Oh, I certainly don't want that." It was both endearing and frustrating that he still remembered my panic that first night we had been together. "I imagine we can get work on that boat you spoke of," I said. "There ought to be some-thing for an enterprising pair like us."

"Yeah. Yeah, we can do that. But no more dead folks on the rise, all right?"

I nodded firmly. "That is an excellent notion. No more mummies."

EPILOGUE

As it turned out, we had a dahabeeyah all to ourselves.

Marion had a dig at Amarna that he wanted us to look into. We told him we were not ready to face more tombs. I could not abide the thought of another confrontation with some horrific dead creature in an enclosed space.

"Never fear, dear boy," he'd said. "There are temples. Out in the open. No monsters."

"I could get used to this living-on-a-boat thing," Eric said on our third night out. The breeze blew softly, the stars shone, and the night was cool and sweet.

"You could, hmm?" I turned away from the rail to look at him, standing there in his shirtsleeves, arms crossed over his chest. "I rather like it myself."

The best part of it was that, aside from the crew and Reis Abdullah, we had no one to watch us.

"Wanna go in, lover?"

His hand cupped my bottom before sliding between my legs, and I gasped, nodding. I had become too accustomed to him, no doubt.

Our suite on the boat was beautifully appointed in the art nouveau style, but the best part about it was the large bed, bolted to the floor. We had already tested it many times, so Eric knew full well it could take the strain of lifting me and tossing me upon it.

I laughed, bouncing a bit, holding my arms open for him.

He came down on me, kissing me madly, taking my breath. His clever fingers worked my clothes open, laying me bare for him. He kissed me from top to bottom and back again, laving each bit of skin with his tongue. My chin, my nipples, and my belly received special attention. Then he moved to my cock, licking it from tip to base.

"Eric!"

"Love the way you taste," he murmured before taking me in his mouth and sucking.

When I could take no more, I pulled him up to me and kissed him, tasting myself there, tiny, salty drops that I sucked off his tongue. He opened his trousers and moved against me, our pricks lining up so sweetly that we both gasped.

"Need you, lover. Need you so bad."

"How? I am yours."

"In me."

This was a special joy, one I could not resist, and I turned us, putting him on his back and bending to set my mouth between his spread legs. I licked behind his balls, then pressed my mouth to his tiny entrance, making him cry out my name over and over. I opened him with my tongue, sliding it in and out in an approximation of what I would do with my prick, driving him higher and higher.

His balls pressed my chin, his cock rubbed my cheek, and when two fingers could slide in and out easily along with my tongue, I rose above him and slicked my cock with my own spit.

"Now, Chrissy. Christian. Now."

"Yes. Now." He was so beautiful I could barely stand it, his gray eyes shining for me, his hands opening and closing on the sheets. His face was set in hard, needy lines, and I took a kiss as I pressed inside him, feeling his body close around me like a vise.

I thrust into him, filling him until my hips met his arse, and then we moved together in perfect concert. He clutched at me with his hands, pulling me down to share a wild kiss, our teeth pressing our lips until we bled.

His cock rubbed my belly, wet and hot, and I reached between us to grasp it, my thumb digging against his slit. Only a few more strokes had him coming, his cry loud, bursting from his chest.

I took my time, thrusting hard the last few times, spending deep within him as he so often did within me. Filling him.

"God, I love you. You're coming back to the States with me when the season is over, lover."

My heart should have been slowing, but it set up a heavy beat instead. "Am I?"

"Uh-huh. Not letting you go."

"I love you as well."

That was all I really needed to say, I thought. When we had sprinkled the ashes of the king into the Nile the day before, I had decided that love had won the day.

Now, looking at the tiny gold statue of Osiris that sat on the dresser across from the bed, I thought loving Lawless might just sustain my need for adventure for the rest of my life.

WANT MORE?

Julia Talbot

Join the Spurs and Shifters Newsletter for free stories, news, and contests from Julia Talbot and BA Tortuga!

https://lp.constantcontact.com/su/A9CRUzp/baandjulia

AFTERWORD

Hey, folks!

Thanks so much for reading my book! I'm so glad you made it here. If you liked the book, I hope you'll consider leaving a rating or review at your retailer of choice or adding the book to your Goodreads shelf.

If you're interested in more of my books, or in news about when they come out and what's coming soon, please check out my Facebook Group https://www.facebook.com/groups/juliatalbot/ or my newsletter here: https://lp.constantcontact.com/su/A9CRUzp/baandjulia

XXOO and Keep reading!

Julia Talbot

ABOUT THE AUTHOR

Julia Talbot lives in the great Southwest, where there is hot and cold running rodeo, cowboys, and everything from meat and potatoes to the best Tex-Mex. A full-time author, Julia is a hybrid author, published by presses like Dreamspinner and Changeling, as well as indie. She believes that everyone deserves a happy ending, so she writes about love without limits, where boys love boys, girls love girls, and boys and girls get together to get wild, especially when her crazy paranormal characters are involved. Visit Julia's website: http://www.juliatalbot.com/

ALSO BY JULIA TALBOT

Nose to Tail, Inc.

Wolf Manny

Wolf's Man Friday

Wolf Maneuvers

Apex Investigations Series

Fox and Wolf

Jaguar and Grizzly

Mountain Lion and Bobcat

Alpha and Bear

Dead and Breakfast Series

Fangs and Catnip

Fangs for the Memories

Home for the Holidays

Alpha Tales Series

An Alpha in Sheep's Clothing

Packmate for Hire

Too Many Alphas

The Grizzly List

Bear Wanted

One and Only Bear

Bearly Working